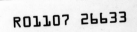

SENTRY IN THE NIGHT

Sentry in the Night

A STORY OF THE AMERICAN REVOLUTION

BY

CHARLES G. WILSON

ILLUSTRATED BY FRANK J. MURCH

IVES WASHBURN, INC.
NEW YORK

PRINTED IN THE UNITED STATES OF AMERICA

VAN REES PRESS   •   NEW YORK

jW6915 se

To my brother
Ian, who heard
the first of these
stories.

CONTENTS

1	A Fight	3
2	An Old Story	8
3	An Arrest	15
4	An "Enlistment"	22
5	A Plot	34
6	A Plot's Failure	45
7	A Voyage	52
8	A New Country	60
9	An Omen	70
10	A First Battle	79
11	A Fire	89
12	A Forced Journey	96
13	A Battle on a Hill	108
14	Surprise at the Tavern	125
15	Guarding an Outpost	138
16	Death in the Snow	149
17	Captivity and Campaigns	161
18	Another Prisoner	174
19	A Journey to the Unknown	181
20	An Enemy's Return	192
21	A Resolution	202
	Author's Note	213

SENTRY IN THE NIGHT

1

A FIGHT

THE big fist, and behind it the wrist covered with coarse red hair, came lazily at Johann as though appearing from a deep mist, a cloud that hid Hantzle's brawny arms, his big body.

Behind him Johann heard a warning shout:

"Duck! Duck, Johann!"

Somehow, though his every muscle ached, though his tattered shirt stuck wetly to him—and all he could think of was how nice it would be to lie down in the play-yard dust—he ducked.

"Now! Now! Give it to him!" It was another voice crying harshly from somewhere outside the cloud. Summoning the last of his waning strength, Johann struck out blindly, as hard as his wiry, seventeen-year-old body knew how. He felt his own fist hit something. Something hard, wet, and hot. Dimly he heard a roar about him, heard a cry of pain, felt himself falling.

When he opened his eyes, the mist had dissolved. He found himself gazing around at a forest of legs and feet. Raising his eyes, he saw looming above him a host of heads and faces. Some were anxious. Some were grinning. The largest grin was on the freckled face of his best friend and school ally, Franz Kottmann.

He saw Franz's lips move, faintly heard his words:

"You did it, Johann! You did it! You beat that bully Hantzle!"

Johann closed his eyes. For a second he forgot his aches. Beaten Hantzle! At last he'd done it! Then he thought, but what's happened to him? I must see how he looks, beaten at last. But the quick short feeling of triumph was lost the minute he tried to rise.

His left arm felt as though a knife blade was jabbing it. Johann wondered whether he'd broken it in the first half of the tussle on the playground. Though his breath came more easily now, it reminded him that he hurt in every fiber. Once more he tried to rise, sank back, closed his burning eyes.

In the next instant he heard the rattle of pebbles, felt the sting of flying earth on his hot face. He opened his eyes to find the onlookers disappearing, legs pumping as hard as their owners could make them go. But Johann didn't need to use his eyes to tell why.

"At it again, eh, my fine young gentleman?"

That voice. There was no other like it. There was only one Dr. Alfred Saxe, head of the school. Nor was there any doubt to whom he addressed his question in his quick, precise tones.

Gritting his teeth against the ache in his arm, Johann first got to his knees, then finally stood shakily erect before a frowning schoolmaster.

"Yes, Herr Doctor," Johann heard himself saying. His voice sounded scratchy and far away. He did not dare raise his eyes from the ancient dark green coat with its familiar decoration of the Emperor in the lapel.

The old, cracked black boots, the gray, patched breeches—no need to look at them, either. None at the *altschule* in Cassel had ever seen Dr. Saxe in any other clothes.

"Well, Johann Leonhardt," the Doctor began. He rolled out the name in his drillmaster fashion. Johann began to tremble anew. "What is it this time? Why were you fighting with Hantzle again?"

Now Johann dared to lift his eyes to the lined, weather-beaten face with its deep-set brown eyes under the shaggy brows. They were eyes that never seemed to move, that bored through his own.

"Well, Johann," he said. "I'm waiting. Why?"

The words fairly gushed out. "He taunted me, Herr Doctor. He's done it before, as you know. I just couldn't let him do it any more. So . . . so we fought."

5

Johann paused, then quickly added: "And I beat him fairly. I beat him, Doctor Saxe!"

The brown eyes were unblinking. "Go on," Dr. Saxe commanded. But even as he told his story, the boy remembered that it wasn't a new one to the schoolmaster. For it wasn't the first fight he'd had with Hantzle. Always, they fought over the same thing. For Hantzle, of all the lads at the school—Johann never knew why—went out of his way to bring up the old story about Johann's father.

"Ha, Leonhardt," was his stock challenge. "Hear anything from that father of yours yet? When is he going to bring back that fortune from America?" A remark usually followed by a derisive laugh and gestures.

Now Johann felt it was one thing to be an orphan and to live on the charity of his elderly aunt; but always, when Hantzle reminded him of how he had been orphaned, or hinted that his father was not all he might have been, Johann was maddened to the core. Hantzle was bigger and older, in fact, two forms ahead of Johann. But he had early learned the secret of goading the younger boy into a lightning fury. And so they fought—often.

And always—until today—with the same result: Johann lost. Maybe now, he thought as he stood before the schoolmaster, Hantzle will cease his tormenting.

"You know the rules here, Johann Leonhardt," said Dr. Saxe, taking a big blue handkerchief from his coat. He dabbed at the perspiration rolling down beneath the three-cornered hat. "I've warned you before about

6

fighting. Now you'll have to take the consequences. Come with me to Herr Gottfriend's office, now."

With that he turned on his heel and went striding down the brick walk to the iron entrance gate.

"But, but, Doctor Saxe," Johann began. "Doctor Saxe . . . I . . ."

No response from the stolid little figure marching along as though he was still on the Emperor's parade ground. The boy saw it would be futile to argue. So he followed behind, pulling the tatters of his shirt together as best he could, tugging at the drooping knees of his soiled and bedraggled breeches. Johann was half-conscious that from behind every linden tree, behind every bush or corner, eyes were following the procession to the gate.

The October wind blew fitfully in the leaves. Johann was grateful for its sudden chill on his bruised and heated body. But more grateful when he heard Franz call:

"Good luck, Johann! And remember, you beat Hantzle!"

He turned to look for Franz. But the school grounds appeared to lie deserted in the autumn sun. The hills above the river behind the school's buildings never seemed more beautiful. His eyes filled with sudden tears. Maybe . . . maybe he'd never come back again to this old school at Cassel!

2

AN OLD STORY

JOHANN had been sitting in Lawyer Gottfriend's dusty old second-floor office opposite Cassel's town hall long enough to see the carved figures on the town clock go around twice—marking a full hour—before he heard chairs scrape in the inner office.

He tried to sit more erect on the hard, worn chair. Maybe Dr. Saxe or Herr Gottfriend, the lawyer, would come out now. His arm still pained him as he tried to pull himself to a more upright position. But even though it still hurt, he smiled to himself as he recollected how he felt when his fist struck against Hantzle's dirty, wet, red face.

What would Herr Gottfriend say this time? As he looked around the little book-cluttered outer office with its battered table and unswept floor, at the familiar picture of the Landgrave of Hesse-Cassel, it seemed to Johann that all the turning points in his young life involved a visit to this withered cubbyhole.

He dimly recollected coming to it with his mother, now only a vaguely remembered figure. He recalled how she cried when she had first brought him to the old lawyer's office; how she had hugged him hard when she came back through the dingy brown wood door.

Then there was the time when the lawyer brought Johann to the office himself. A wet, cold afternoon, at the end of a wet, cold, dismal day, the day his mother had been buried at the little churchyard outside Cassel's walls. It was the lawyer who then told Johann he would henceforth live with an aunt he scarcely knew.

Seven or eight years had passed since his last visit. On that occasion Aunt Frieda had brought him. He was too old to stay longer at a school run by women. It was time he entered an institution with boys of his own age, she had said.

Under Dr. Saxe the discipline had been strict, the food meager at best, and the lessons only those rudiments that any boy of his age might expect to need in Hesse-Cassel in the 1770's. But he made friends, particularly with the butcher's son, Franz, and time passed pleasantly enough—except for Hantzle and his taunts.

The discipline was not much different than that in

9

any school of the age. One of a dozen little "countries" in a greater territory sometimes called "Germany," Hesse-Cassel had its ups and downs. With some rulers, or "landgraves," as they were called, it prospered. Then there was food enough for most. If ill fortune frowned and a less able man ruled, the winters seemed to be longer and colder; the beggars greater in number; the fuel scarcer than anyone ever remembered before.

And always it seemed there was a coming and going of armies in Hesse-Cassel. Not that the country was at war. It was only that brothers and fathers, uncles and cousins were well versed in the art of war in Hesse-Cassel. And always the Landgrave had need of their services—to fight someone else's war. There was hardly a corner of Europe in which some of its citizens hadn't fought.

But now the chairs in the inner office scraped again. The voices grew louder. Surely, they must be coming out now! The old clock across the town square boomed out the hour: one, two, three, four.

Dr. Saxe came out first. He was mopping his brow again with that blue handkerchief. Now he looked at Johann as he put his well-worn hat back on his white-haired head.

"The Herr Lawyer will see you now," he said. "He will tell you what we've decided." Dr. Saxe walked slowly toward the outer door, his hand fumbling for his pocket. He turned around.

"Good-by, Johann. And try to be a better boy." Then he was gone.

"Good-by"! What did he mean, thought Johann.

Through the now open door of the inside office he saw Herr Gottfriend just lowering himself into his big chair behind the piled-up desk. His bald head caught a ray of sun through a side window. Now that head flashed as he motioned Johann to enter.

"Sit down over there, boy," said the little lawyer. The deep, booming voice coming from such a small body always surprised Johann. Now Herr Gottfriend brushed his ink-stained fingers nervously across the lace at his collar.

"I hear you've been in trouble again," he said.

Johann told him the story of his fight and of what had brought it about. "But I don't think he'll make any more trouble for me," he finished hurriedly.

The blue eyes flashed for a minute. Then Herr Gott-friend said softly:

"Neither will you, Johann Leonhardt. Not at the *altschule,* anyway."

"What do you mean, sir?" Johann asked.

"I mean what I say. You've had your last fight at school in Cassel. Doctor Saxe is determined upon that. And so . . ." He picked up a quill pen, fluttered it a bit, and added, "and so you've ended your days there."

Images of Dr. Saxe, Franz, Hantzle, a host of others he knew as pupils, the old brick buildings, the towering trees, whirled through Johann's bewildered mind.

"But what . . . what's to become of me, sir?" he questioned.

"We'll see," said the lawyer. "We'll see, Johann Leon-hardt. Meanwhile, I want to tell you something . . .

11

something that may have a bearing on 'what's to become' of you."

Stunned, Johann watched the ray of sunshine as it crept up over the top of the bald head, over the rows of dusty law books, to the top of the bookcases, where he knew, almost without looking, rested the plaster busts of Homer, Plato, and Luther. His eyes came back to the lawyer. He was crinkling a bit of paper in his lean fingers.

"Listen. Listen carefully, Johann Leonhardt, to what I am going to tell you now. For reasons best known to myself I've never said anything to you about your family. But now . . . now when you seem to have arrived willy-nilly at a new path in your life, I feel I should hold it from you no longer."

Outside, the clock struck the half-hour. The spot of sunlight had disappeared. A cold chill made Johann shiver in his sweat-soaked, torn shirt.

"Your father, Wilhelm Leonhardt, you must know," began the lawyer, "was the younger son of a onetime wealthy merchant here in Cassel. Your grandfather would have nothing to do with him after he married your mother, a fine woman, but one your grandfather felt beneath his son. When he died, your grandfather cut off your father without a thaler.

"Stung by this act, shunned by the rest of his family, your father tried to make the best of circumstances here in Cassel. But nothing he tried succeeded. Then, after you were born, he decided to try his hand at making a new life in the colonies of England, across the Atlantic in the new land called America.

12

"Nothing was heard of him for years. Your mother, a gentle woman, pined away and finally died, heartbroken. Then, two years ago through a client of mine with connections in this America—in the town of New York, once called New Amsterdam when the Dutch held it before the English—I learned your father had made a modest fortune as a ship's outfitter. Unfortunately, however, my client's friend informed me, your father died almost on the eve of his sending for you and your mother. He, of course, was unaware of her death."

Outside the clock tolled again. The evening shadows began to fall thickly in the office. Johann heard the birds, disturbed by the clock's strokes, fluttering through the still air outside. The lawyer went on:

"You must know that this America I tell you of is a vast, almost empty place, teeming, they tell me, with natural riches, the land just waiting for a hand to turn it to advantage. That's the kind of land your father received through the generosity of a sea captain he once befriended, if the story they tell me be true. He did some favor for this man and was given the deed to some land near the mountains, the Alleghenies, I believe they call them.

"Legally, and rightfully," went on Herr Gottfriend, "that property is now yours. But the strangest part of this story I now tell you. For some reason not clear to me, the deed is etched in the back of the case of an old watch the sea captain gave your father. No paper deed ever passed hands, so that the only proof is contained in the watch case. My client's friend relates that when your father died he left the watch in charge of a dear friend.

13

That man still holds the watch. There is only one way you can now assert your claim to your father's estate and to the property. That is by physically going to New York and claiming the watch."

Now the office was all but pitch black. The outline of the windows was clear, but Lawyer Gottfriend's face was deep in shadow. Trembling, Johann sat silent, frightened but hopeful of what the old lawyer might say next. He rustled some of his papers with a suddenness that made Johann jump, then added:

"That's why I said when I started that what I should tell you would have a bearing on 'what's to become' of you. You see, Johann, you just can't pick up at the age of seventeen and go to America. It will take a bit of planning. It will take time to hit upon the best way of doing it. So now, go home to your Aunt Frieda. Say nothing of what I've told you, for even she knows nothing of your father's death. And come here early tomorrow morning, and we'll talk about it further."

The square was dark and all but deserted when Johann came down the worn steps, his head brimming with the lawyer's story. What would Herr Gottfriend decide upon? How would he ever get to this America across the ocean? Were the Alleghenies higher than the hills that surrounded the river town?

These thoughts and half a hundred others ran through his mind as he hurried along, his aches and the chill of the evening forgotten. And I'll be late for supper if I don't walk faster still, thought Johann.

14

3

AN ARREST

THE following morning Johann went to Herr Gottfriend's office—but as early as he arrived, the old lawyer
was there before him.

"Good morning, Johann," he boomed. "That's one
virtue I'm glad to see you have. You can be prompt.
But to business. It will take some time to plan the way
in which we will go about recovering your heritage.
Meanwhile, I propose you work for me here in my
office. A healthy lad like yourself should be useful for
something more than punching his schoolmates."

Thus it was that he began running errands, sorting innumerable papers, and keeping the old man's rooms reasonably tidy. After the strict discipline of the *altschule,* his freedom to roam the city's streets seemed wonderful. Not a week passed but Herr Gottfriend sent him on some trip or other. To another lawyer's office, to the courts—and sometimes—to the old stone jail.

Johann had just come out of that gloomy building one day when he heard shouts down the street. Looking in that direction, he saw they came from a group of people struggling slowly toward where he stood.

Two of the town's constables were half dragging, half carrying between them a tall, powerful-looking youth. Behind, beside, and all around the officers marched the shouting, gesturing throng. Their angry cries now came plainly to Johann.

"Let him go! Let him go! Do you hear me?" he heard a woman cry.

"Yes! Yes! Release him! He's not the one you want!" cried one of the men.

Then, as the crowd pressed closer, one of the constables loosened his hold on the youth, raised his staff, and swung it in a wide arc around him. One of the men fell to the paving stones and lay there writhing. At that the noise from the crowd redoubled, but, unheeding, the constables resumed their progress.

The barred gates behind Johann suddenly swung open, and the officers hustled their prisoner inside. Johann caught a brief glimpse of the lad's face. It was pale where it wasn't scratched or bleeding. His blond hair was tousled, his eyes wild with fear. Then he and his captors were shut behind the big gates.

It was the first time Johann had seen anyone hustled off to the jail. His previous visits to the jail assured him the building was well filled—but it came as a shock to him nonetheless. What had the boy done? Why were these people so angry?

Now as he looked at them, he saw several of the men gathering around one of the women. She was crying as though her heart would break. Though Herr Gottfriend had warned Johann against loitering and meddling in the affairs of others, he could not restrain his curiosity. He had to find out what had brought on this strange episode.

Johann decided to speak to an elderly, poorly dressed fellow, one of two standing somewhat apart from the throng.

"Excuse me, sir," he began. "But I have to know. Why did the constable take that boy?"

The man whirled with a belligerent air that made Johann suddenly wish he hadn't asked him the question. The old man's mouth worked as though he couldn't find words; his smudged face screwed itself into a fearful scowl.

"Why? Why, you asked? That's a question now, isn't it?" And, turning to his companion growled, "Hear this one, Jacob. He wants to know why those dogs took our Peter!"

Johann's face flushed; he grew hot all over as, at the loudly spoken words, half of those in the crowd turned their eyes on him.

17

"What business is it of yours?" shrilled one of the women.

"Yes! 'Tis too bad it wasn't you they took! You look young enough and sturdy enough to shoulder a gun!" said another.

"Not him they wouldn't," rejoined the man Johann had first spoken to, his voice sounding like a trumpet in the now quiet street. "Look at him." The words were scornful. "Look. Wavy blond hair. Blue eyes and milk-white skin. They know what they want." He paused, then added, gratingly, mockingly: "Men. Real men. Men like our Peter!"

Johann felt his heart begin to pound furiously; his blood raced in his veins, just as it had when Hantzle taunted him.

But something told him it would do no good to quarrel with the sooty-faced man. Instead, he decided to forget his curiosity and leave quietly. But just then the man addressed as "Jacob," who up to now hadn't said a word, approached Johann.

"I'm sorry, lad, that my friend the blacksmith here seems so hasty-tempered. But indeed he has reason, as have the rest of these good people."

His voice, his clothes—especially the fine-shaped hat and the silver buckles on his shoes—made it clear to Johann he was a man of some consequence.

"You see," he went on, "the youth the constables took is the nephew of this worthy blacksmith, Hans Zengher. He runs a blacksmith shop over on Braun-strasser. Hans and these others are angry because Peter

18

has been seized as a 'substitute' for a deserter from Colonel von Holzen's regiment."

"But what's he done?" insisted Johann.

"Nothing," replied Jacob, "except that God made him tall, strapping, and healthy. So, when a man in the district where the smithy lies deserted a week ago, the people were compelled to furnish someone to take his place in the Landgrave's army."

"You mean he had to go whether he wanted to or not?" asked Johann.

Jacob half smiled. "You must either be younger than you look—or else haven't lived around here long enough to know how the Landgrave, our gracious master, gets the men to fight in his armies." Then, moving farther away from the blacksmith, he beckoned to Johann to step aside with him.

"You must know," began Jacob, "that our little realm of Hesse-Cassel is just one of hundreds in a larger area, called by some Germany. Each is ruled by a duke, a prince, or a king. Our ruler, of course, is Frederick II, Landgrave of Hesse-Cassel.

"Our people are mostly farmers. We don't produce many things that we can sell to neighboring countries. But we have a healthy climate, and many and many a tall, well-built lad like yourself in our few square miles.

"So it has come about that to make use of some of our men, our rulers have, for centuries, 'loaned' them to other, larger nations to help them fight their battles. Some countries may trade in crops and manufactured goods. We trade in men, it might be said.

"Back in 1687 the then Landgrave 'loaned' an army

19

to the people of Venice to fight the Turks; some of our 'hired' armies fought in Italy; others in an invasion of England. It seems it has always been so in Hesse-Cassel." He stopped, sighed, and looked back at the people still standing in front of the jail.

"I remember one time a group of lads—and oldsters, too—were sent off. A few, more daring than the others, questioned why they were being sent out to fight in another country's cause. But they didn't live long enough to get an answer, for their commanding officer ordered them shot—while the rest of the men 'recruited' shouted, 'Hurrah!'

"I'll never forget that—or what followed. As they marched along, some crying, some white-faced, children ran along beside fathers; husbands were forced from the arms of their wives. And even old men who had seen this before got so angry that they threw their crutches at the marching men. And all through it, I remember, the drums, the rolling of the drums. Then, just as they passed through the gates of the city, some of them turned and shouted: 'God save you, wife! God keep you, child! Long live the Landgrave! We'll be back for the Judgment Day!' "

Jacob explained to Johann how the country was cut up into districts, each required to raise a given number of recruits for a certain regiment. Boys of seventeen were as likely to be called as men of fifty and older. Under these circumstances, he went on, desertion from the army was common. The law said that when a deserter was announced from a district, its people must rise and occupy the roads, paths, and bridges for a whole day, or until the fugitive was caught.

"But if he is not caught," Johann asked, "what happens?"

"Then lads like Peter must suffer the consequences. The district is required by law to supply an able-bodied man to take his place. That's how and why they took Peter Zengher in. Now Hans will be alone in his blacksmith shop—and, goodness knows, may never see Peter again."

Johann looked again at the crowd. Although he knew none of them, he felt for them in their trouble. Then a thought came to him.

"Mr. Jacob," he said, "maybe my master, Herr Gottfriend, could help Peter and Hans." He explained that the old lawyer often was able to get people released from jail.

Jacob patted him gently on the shoulder. "You're a kindhearted lad, and I thank you for the thought. But where Peter's going, no lawyer will do any good. Once they get their clutches on a man, there's no easy way out—short of a bullet, that is." And he walked back to rejoin the blacksmith and his crying wife.

Johann returned to the office, wondering. Why did such things happen in a peaceful town like Cassel? Why was it that the Landgrave could be so cruel to his people? What would poor Hans do now? And would Peter live to return to Cassel and the smithy?

4

AN "ENLISTMENT"

JOHANN'S days as an assistant passed quickly and profitably. As he gained the old man's confidence, he was given more responsible tasks. He even tried to make some sense out of the big law books. But in his heart, Johann longed for the word that would start him toward the land across the sea.

He never wearied of asking questions about this country. How big was it? Were there many people from the Old World living there? Was it true there were immense forests, larger than any in all of Hesse-Cassel?

When Herr Gottfriend felt so disposed, he could tell many things about this America across the broad Atlantic. How it had been claimed and conquered in part by many nations—Spain, England, and France. And how finally England, largely with the aid of her people who had settled there, had won control of most of the land from France only a few years before in the "Seven Years' War."

"But even now," the lawyer told him, "there is no telling what may happen any day over there. You see, the people have lived practically under their own rule for so long, and are so far removed from the mother country, they resent any English interference with their lives and laws."

Indeed, he explained, rebellion had already broken out in Massachusetts, one of the English colonies. The people of the colony had, a few months before, come to an open clash of arms with soldiers sent by the English king to put down the clamor for freedom from unjust taxation.

"The first shots were fired at a place called Lexington," he said. "Last June, after the King's soldiers won a battle at Bunker Hill, the colonists, under a general named George Washington, hemmed the soldiers in by laying siege to Boston, the principal town in Massachusetts."

Then one day Herr Gottfriend received news from his client's friend in New York. He wrote he would appreciate some action by Johann toward an early claiming of his father's property. Herr Gottfriend showed Johann the letter.

"Things are pretty well stirred up over here now," it read. "And since no one knows what will come of this rebellion against the King, I advise that you send young Leonhardt here as soon as possible." The letter was signed "Joseph Crainter," and dated in New York, August 16, 1775.

Within the week, the old lawyer told Johann he had arranged for him to sail. By early spring, he said, Johann should be in America!

The new year, 1776, came in, and Johann did his work with ill-concealed impatience. Every time he went on some errand he thought: "Perhaps this is the last one! Maybe tomorrow I'll sail for New York!"

Then, one morning late in January, when the lawyer called Johann into his office, the boy felt surely this was to be the big day. But as he entered, he noticed Herr Gottfriend seemed graver than usual.

"Sit down," he said. "I've news for you." He paused. "But I'm afraid its bad news." He looked quickly at Johann to see how he would take the announcement. The boy's heart sank. What could have happened? Slowly, the old man picked up a gazette from his desk and began to read:

"The subjects of the Landgrave of Hesse-Cassel learned last week that a treaty had been signed with the King of Great Britain, George III. By this treaty, the Landgrave agrees to furnish, this year of 1776, twelve thousand or more fully equipped soldiers for the service of Great Britain in the North American provinces, where a rebellion is now in progress against the British

24

King. Recruitment of the necessary men will begin within the week.

"The subjects of the Landgrave are assured this will not only add another honor to those that have already fallen on his soldiers and army, but will mean the heavy burden of taxation will be lightened. For the Landgrave has made it known that for every soldier furnished, his Treasury will be paid about £7."

"But, but," Johann stammered, "why should that be bad news for me?"

"It means," answered the lawyer, "that a young lad like yourself will not be allowed to leave the country now. The Prince will need every man he can get to fulfill his treaty." Herr Gottfriend looked away a minute, then added. " 'Tis a bad business." He sighed deeply and half to himself said: "But it's always been that way in Hesse-Cassel."

Very soon Johann saw plenty of evidence of the Landgrave's intention to carry out his word to the British King. Everywhere recruitment signs appeared. Men in uniform—the blue and white of the Guards regiments or the black of the Fusiliers—went about telling men of the town how they could gain wealth and renown by joining the army.

"This country," Johann heard one of them say, "is all but a-swim in milk and honey. Lots of land. Lots of pretty girls. Fine homes. And the clods who live there now didn't know any better than to rebel against their king. Come with us when we cross the sea, and you'll not regret it."

And almost daily the scenes that Mr. Jacob had described took place as men were hastily marched away to a training center. Some, it was easy to see, were eager to go, anxious for a quick war and quick wealth. But others, mostly older men, went unwillingly. It must be these that make it necessary to have so many guards march with them to camp, thought Johann.

The winter drew to a close, and on one of the first warm days in March, Herr Gottfriend told Johann he was going to send him on a few days' journey to the town of Bach.

"Here are the papers you are to take with you," he said. "You'd best take a change of linen, for you'll be gone three or four days. And here," he reached into his money box, "are ten thalers for your trip." Then, after rummaging through the pile of papers on his desk, he handed Johann a letter. "This will serve you as identification, in case anybody questions your right to be out of Cassel at this time."

Johann enjoyed every moment of his bumpy ride in the post coach to Bach. To a lad who had lived all his life in Cassel, the sight of new villages, different rivers, and the customs at posting inns were exciting. He had some trouble finding the right address in the crooked streets of the old town, but having delivered the papers, discovered he had plenty of time before the return coach left.

So he used it to tramp all about Bach, taking in the sights, buying a trinket for his aunt, then returned to the coaching inn, tired, cold, and hungry. He seated himself at one of the tables in the big common room and soon was savoring a juicy meat pie, enjoying meanwhile the heat from the huge fireplace. Not more than a half-dozen others were in the room, some, like himself, waiting for the coach. Suddenly the door banged open.

Through it stepped two tall grenadiers, fully armed. Behind them walked an officer, so tall he had to duck his high, brass-faced helmet to enter. Immediately all conversation in the room came to a halt. Johann felt his heart begin to beat rapidly. What did they want? He didn't have to wait long to find out.

For, after removing his helmet, the officer, in a voice that rang through the low-raftered room, began to read from a paper he held in his hand.

"Whereas, it has pleased his Highness, the Landgrave of Hesse-Cassel, to offer aid to George III, King of Great Britain in order to bring peace to the rebellious subjects of the American provinces, it is hereby. . . ."

The rest of his proclamation was lost in the crash of a table. One of the men in the room now rose quickly, stepped past the fallen furniture, and turned toward the stairs.

Instantly there were two sharp snaps as the soldiers brought their guns to a level position, aiming them directly at the silent and wondering inn guests.

"Take that dog!" the officer shouted.

The man stopped in his tracks and faced about. In the firelight's gleam Johann saw his face, white and drawn.

"But, Herr Captain," he said, "You can't take me. I'm a free citizen of Worms, here on business. See," and he fumbled in his coat, "here are my identification

27

papers. All in order." Shakily, he held them out to one of the grenadiers.

The soldier tore them from his grasp, took a quick look, ripped them in two, and threw the pieces on the floor. Next, he spun the man about and shoved him toward the other soldier.

"Take him outside, quick!" ordered the officer, at the same time glancing stonily at the rest in the room.

"Yes, my Captain," responded the soldier. Seizing the man from Worms in an iron grip between them, the soldiers hustled him out the still open inn door.

Two more soldiers entered as soon as the others had left.

"Examine all of these curs!" ordered the officer. "The Landgrave has need of men now! We can't waste all night here!"

In rapid succession every man was ordered to show his identification. The papers of an older tradesman were given a bare glance, then tossed to the dirty, sand-strewn floor. "You can go," said the examining soldier to this man. And to the officer, the soldier added: "He's no good, my Captain." The officer, standing in front of the fire warming himself never looked up but just shrugged his shoulders and stepped closer to the blaze.

Now it was Johann's turn. "Oh, a fine, ruddy lad, I'll warrant me," said the grenadier as he advanced toward the boy. The firelight shimmered on his helmet as he stood, towering above Johann, hand outstretched for his papers.

"A lawyer's clerk, Captain," the soldier shouted.

"From Cassel, it says here. He looks a bit on the soft side though. Shall we take him?"

"*Dummkopf*," snapped the officer with hardly a glance at Johann. "Don't ask such silly questions. Take him outside with those others. He'll do. Lots of spirit— if I can only see it. But he'll do."

With a careless toss of his big hand, the soldier threw Johann's papers onto the fire. They flared up and became no more than a charred mass amid the bright coals.

"All right, young one," grinned the soldier. "Captain says you'll do. I won't argue with him. Now, march."

Then for the first time Johann found words. "But my master," he cried. "My master won't hear of it! What will I tell him? How will he know what's happened to me?"

"Oh, we'll tell him all about you," mocked the officer. "Won't we, Mertz? We'll tell him how you volunteered to serve the Landgrave. That's right, isn't it, Mertz?"

"Of course we will, sonny." The soldier imitated his captain's tone. "Now, get along out there. You're keeping some good recruits waiting!" And in a minute Johann found himself in the street in front of the inn where about a dozen men huddled under the watchful eyes of six or seven soldiers.

"Here's another 'volunteer'!" shouted Johann's guard. And he was propelled forward so rapidly that he bumped squarely into the waiting knot of men.

Now it was getting dark. The biting wind felt all

29

the more chilly for the time spent in toasting before the inn's warm fire. Johann's teeth chattered for all the churning rage inside his breast. To be treated this way—papers torn up—hustled into an army he didn't wish to join—no chance to tell his friends or his aunt! Had he no rights at all?

As he looked about, he saw his companions were shivering just as he was. Then one of them suddenly spoke. He was a heavy-set, middle-aged fellow. His words fairly rasped out:

"I'll warrant me the King of England would feel he'd been swindled could he but see what he got for his seven pounds in you." And he glowered at Johann.

For the moment, Johann forgot about the cold, about leaving his half-finished supper so unceremoniously, at the injustice of his position. Anger brought warmth to his cheeks and to his tongue:

"I didn't ask to come. If the King of England's been cheated, 'tis his own fault—or at least that officer's!"

"Well spoken, lad," said another in the group. In the faint light from the inn, he appeared to be a man in his early forties, tall and spare, but decently dressed as though a tradesman of some sort. "And you there, with the rusty-gate voice have had your answer, or Ziggner's not my name." This he said in turning from Johann to face the first speaker. His eyes returned to Johann as he added, "Never mind, boy. He's just jealous that he isn't getting the seven pounds himself instead of our esteemed Landgrave."

For all their plight, the others burst into a laugh when they heard this retort. The rasping-voiced man appeared to hear none of it, but looked steadily toward the inn as though impatient to be on his way to wherever the soldiers wanted to take them.

"None o' us asked to come for that matter," volunteered another in the group. "I'd give 'em five times seven pounds if they'd leave me go home."

"Aye, an' seven times seven pounds," put in a third man. "Blast 'em!"

" 'Specially the King of Great Britain!" rejoined a fourth. "What's he want o' me, anyways?"

"Quiet! Quiet, you recruits!" yelled the stout corporal. "D'ye want to stand here all night in this cold? Pest send the rest o' your kind inside. If they'd make up their minds, we could all be on our way!"

The bare tree limbs swayed in the sharpening night wind. Johann shivered again when he looked through the inn window at the reflection of the cheerful fire inside. The inn door opened, and the officer and soldiers came out.

"That's all we'll get here, Corporal," said the captain, hunching himself deep into his cloak. "March these off to the collecting place. And see that none of them get away, mind you! Forward, march!"

A few prods from the gun barrels and Johann and his companions started down the bare, cold streets toward the guard post and the gate leading to the countryside beyond. Few there were who bothered to leave their firesides to see them go by. Those who opened their doors at the sound of tramping feet shut them quickly when they saw the grenadiers, marching stiffly erect beside the group.

"But, but," said Johann to the man named Ziggner, "don't they care what happens to us?"

"Not them, son," replied the other. "They're just glad they ain't in our shoes."

They marched on in silence, then Ziggner added, "But don't fret, lad. We're all in this together, now, an' you can count on me as a friend."

The darkened buildings sent back the echoes of footsteps on the paving stones as they moved on, each, like Johann, folded deep in his own cold thoughts.

5

A PLOT

"READY! Present! Aim! Fire!"

The ragged volley shattered the frosty air. At its sound a flock of crows rose cawing into the bright, sun-lit March sky.

"You there, Leonhardt," bellowed the corporal. "You're not hunting ducks. Level that piece next time, or, by thunder, you'll spend a few hours on extra duty!"

A month had passed since Johann had been "re-cruited" into a battalion of the Regiment von Knyphausen. A month in which he'd heard little but, "Leonhardt, don't do that!" Or, "Leonhardt, don't do it that way!" A month whose days hardly seemed long enough to learn all there was to a soldier's trade.

The collecting place had turned out to be nothing but a drab group of tumble-down buildings, surrounded by a stout wooden wall with a strong, barred gate. Since arrival, none had seen the outside of that gate. Each of the buildings was just big enough to house a dozen men. Each was drafty, had rough, cracked wooden walls, and a dirt floor. At night the men bedded down like so many cattle in a stall.

But after marching all day to the tap-tap-tap of a drum and the shrilling of a fife, countermarching, learning how to load and fire their guns, Johann and his fellows were only too glad to tumble down on the cold floors and fall asleep, still shivering.

Sometimes, before falling asleep, Johann wondered whether he'd ever be able now to go to New York to claim his inheritance. He tried to picture his father's gold watch with its map of a strange country on the inside of the case. Would be ever get to see it? Would he ever hear from Herr Gottfriend again?

As the weeks wore on, with no word from the old lawyer, Johann began to resign himself to his fate. Johann knew America was a big place, but, he thought, perhaps if I'm really sent across the ocean, I'll get the chance to visit New York.

Soon there was no doubt of the regiment's ultimate purpose. They were going, so the rumor had it, to America as soon as they had finished the training period and had been approved by the British Commissioner who would inspect them before they were shipped. Probably, thought Johann, he has to make sure the British King gets his seven pounds' worth.

Then, as in all armies, the never failing topic of talk was: when do we go? Some, like Baum, the man who had addressed Johann the night they were taken at the inn, had served before. He went about his duties and drill with a minimum of difficulty.

"Donner!" he would say in his rasping tone. "There's nothin' to worry about. Just do what they tell you an' you'll be all right." It was Baum who told long stories about soldiering in foreign lands while they munched their sparse rations of an evening.

"There'll be plenty to be had in this new country," he'd say. "Lots o' wine, lots o' gold, silver, and jewels. To say nothin' about the stuff you can sell after a town is taken.

"Why, I remember once in Italy when we was fightin' for the Duke, I picked up enough stuff in one town to keep me in wine an' money for months. Months, d'ye hear? Lived like a captain, I did. An' from what they tell me o' this America, it should be twice as easy.

"None o' those little towns they have," he continued, "has walls around 'em. We just march up, bang off a few volleys; they'll run away like the bumpkins they are—an' the town'll be ours to do as we please."

But the prospects outlined by Baum did not, Johann noticed, tempt everyone. For example, there was Gorthalman, a stooped, elderly fringemaker from Hanover. He'd settle, he said, for his own town where he had a prosperous business until thrown into the Landgrave's army.

Nor was Kampel pleased, once a civil servant looking forward to retirement on a small pension. A Mainz man, he was close to sixty when the soldiers closed in on him. His pudgy figure drooped visibly under day after day of hard drill.

Another, "Father" Claus, Johann knew, felt much as he did. He had served some time in a monastery near Würzburg. He felt, apparently from his religious training, he must bear his fate without murmuring too loudly. It was hard for Johann to understand how a former monk could adapt himself to a soldier's life. But somehow he did it—and managed always to carry his prayer book about him. Tall, thin, and wiry, for all his sheltered life, Claus stood up well under the rigors of army life.

But there were others who, like Baum, accepted the new existence with no more than the customary complaints about its severity. They saw it as a way out of their civilian difficulties.

Ziggner was one of these. His once-flourishing business had gone bankrupt. He always blamed a crafty partner for his trouble. He reveled in his new surroundings. His skinny frame seemed to thrive on the poor food and the hard work. Ziggner listened more eagerly than anyone to Baum's stories of riches.

In the first few weeks it was Ziggner, too, who, more than the others, listened to Johann's worries and complaints about his enforced service. And it was Ziggner who helped him when a ramrod refused to work as it should, who made sure that the boy was not always elbowed out of the way when the rations were served out.

"Maybe this Baum knows more," he would say, "but it takes one real civilian to understand another. If I can be of any help to you, don't hesitate to ask me."

For all the difference in their ages, Johann began to feel that out of the thousands at the encampment, he had one real friend in Ziggner.

But while he criticized Baum for his attitude of superiority about things military, Ziggner was ever willing to speculate on the tales he told.

"You know," he said to Johann as they rested between drills, "if Baum is right—an' he should know— we ought to be able to make a fortune in America." His thin, lined face with its narrow, dark eyes tightened momentarily as he added: "Then, then I'll come back here an' do for that Klather." Klather was the man who had ruined him, Ziggner explained. Often, he would call out in his sleep, "Now I've got you, Klather! Give it back to me!"

One day after the battalion had been dismissed, the corporal called Johann. "Leonhardt, I've orders to send you over to General von Kohrn's quarters. What you've done now, I don't want to know. But you'd better report, and on the double."

Johann hurried to the General's building, presented himself to the sentry at the door, and was ushered into a well-appointed room. At its end stood a long table backed up to a roaring fire. Seated behind the table, resplendent in a general's uniform, was the largest man

38

Johann had ever seen. His body fairly bulged over the back and arms of the chair. The huge dome of a head was without a wig. The eyes in the shiny red face, perspiring from the fire's heat, glanced up when Johann appeared.

"Leonhardt reporting, sir," Johann said, presenting his gun in salute as smartly as he knew how. But as he did, his trembling hands missed their grip, and the gun's heavy butt crashed to the floor. Quickly he recovered it and stood at attention. All the time the eyes never left Johann's face. The sweating features never moved.

"Oh, Leonhardt." The high-pitched voice hardly seemed to fit the big body. "You were formerly apprenticed to an attorney? That right?"

"Yes, sir," replied Johann.

The General paused, the eyes still boring through the erect figure before him. Then:

"How do you like our army?"

"Why, why," stammered Johann taken aback by such a question from a superior officer, "I like it fine."

"I have a letter from Herr Gottfriend, your old master, speaking very highly of your abilities," continued the General. "Know how to read and write, eh?"

"Yes, sir," said Johann, wondering what the General had in mind.

"Very well, then," he said. "Report here tomorrow after first drill. You'll be assigned as my aide. Tell your corporal you are to be excused from field training. Dismissed." And the big hands pulled on the wig lying on the table. As Johann turned to leave he noticed the wig was slightly askew over one eye.

As an aide, Johann learned how to make up muster rolls, how to make out reports on ammunition, powder, supplies, and to find his way about the encampment carrying messages for the General. The tremendous man with the squeaky voice was kind but exacting, and, as the boy found out, could be just as stern with those who violated regulations as any officer in the camp.

Through his work at the General's quarters, Johann learned more about the treaty the Landgrave had committed himself to. The treaty guaranteeing delivery of the men had been debated at length in the British Parliament.

Some Englishmen had held it shameful that Great Britain should hire mercenaries—as Johann and his fellows were termed—to fight battles with the American colonists. The treaty had been signed, Johann found out, only after the British government had tried, unsuccessfully, to get men from the Empress Catherine of Russia. Those English who favored the idea of hiring soldiers from Hesse-Cassel pointed out that Great Britain, with other wars abroad, could hardly get volunteers from her own people sufficient to provide an army for restoring order in America.

"It's not mine to question orders," Johann heard General von Kohrn say one day to another officer. "But I can't see what should be so hard about putting down a pack of farmers living in a wilderness. They've no training, no stores of ammunition, no ships to prevent an invasion. Why, they tell me their leaders are just weeks off the farm, or out of some clerk's office. How can men like these resist trained troops?"

Although assigned as an aide, Johann still was required to sleep at his own hut. In the weeks since getting his new duties, Johann and his old companions had hardly spoken to each other. The few words he'd had with Ziggner, however, made it clear that he, somehow, seemed to resent Johann's advancement.

One night shortly after the encampment had learned the troops would sail within a few weeks, Johann entered the hut to find its occupants gathered about in a circle, talking loudly and heatedly. But the moment he stepped through the door, the conversation stopped. He sat down on the floor and began to remove his boots, his back turned toward them.

Then he heard Gorthalman say softly: "Go ahead. He's your friend. Ask him." There was a moment of silence, followed by a whispered "All right," then Johann heard Ziggner say loudly:

"Leonhardt, how'd you like to get out of all this?"

Johann turned about, one boot still in his hands. In the faint candle's light he could see now that all the men in the hut were looking intently at him.

Without his uniform coat and helmet, Ziggner now appeared to Johann just like the merchant he used to be—still anxious to please a customer. Gorthalman stood shading his deep-set eyes against the candle's light. Baum, even without boots or headgear, still appeared every inch the soldier. Father Claus, like Kampel, stood silent. Johann looked at them all before he spoke.

"What do you mean, 'get out of all this'?"

Ziggner took a step nearer. "Just what I say. You don't fancy that general's billet of yours so much you want to stay in it, do you? Do you want to be shipped over the ocean? Perhaps buried there? Do you?"

Now Johann could see he was deadly serious. Turning toward Baum again, Johann saw the veteran's eyes were noncommittal. Claus's gaze met Johann's squarely, Kampel stared at the floor, while Gorthalman moved nearer the hut door.

"What's it all about?" cried Johann, alarmed.

"Wait a bit," said Ziggner, "we want to have a few answers. How do you feel about all this?" and he waved his arm to take in the bare, cold hut. "Do you enjoy it so much you'd risk nothing to get out of it? Or," and his voice was scornful, "do you feel because you're the General's aide you're a bit better than the rest of us?"

"You know that's not so," Johann said. "We're all in the same boat as far as I can figure it. You told me that yourself."

"That's what I told you he'd say," broke in Gorthalman. "So did Kampel, here." There was a moment's silence, then he added, "Well, go on. Go on. Tell him, for I'm sure he'll be with us."

Ziggner took a deep breath, tugged nervously at his bayonet belt, and began:

"You know why most of us are here—not because we wanted to be, but because we were forced into it. You've heard—as we have—that we're to sail for America within the fortnight. That means we may never see our homes, our friends, or our families again."

Ziggner took another breath, then continued:

42

"You an' me, all of us here would be glad to fight if our country was bein' invaded. But why should we get mixed up in a quarrel that's no makin' o' ours? Is it because," and he lowered his voice, "our mighty Landgrave wants to give some foreign king some soldiers at seven pounds apiece? The devil with it. The devil, I say, with America an' its riches. An' we say, one an' all, we don't want no easy pickin's. We're gettin' out."

Inwardly amazed, Johann then listened while Ziggner told of the plan he and others in the encampment proposed. Three nights before the regiment was to leave, some hundreds of men who had agreed to the scheme were to rise in the night, disarm the guards, seize their weapons, cut down all who opposed them. Then they would render the cannon harmless, lock up the officers in their quarters, and march away across the nearest border to seek sanctuary in a neighboring country.

As Ziggner's voice droned on, unfolding the plan, Johann's head filled with conflicting thoughts. What had caused Ziggner's sudden change? He had never so much as mentioned his dissatisfaction to Johann. What had happened to Ziggner's ambitions to go along with the army to recoup his fortunes in the New World? The tall ex-tradesman hardly seemed to be the same person Johann had come to know in the first few weeks at the encampment.

One voice within Johann argued that Ziggner might be right. To revolt and escape was really the only way to avoid a nameless fate in a wild, faraway country. But another voice quickly answered, how else are you,

Johann Leonhardt, going to get to this America and get your father's estate and the watch?

Ziggner was still talking, the gesturings of his head reflected in the shadow on the wall of the hut. But how, thought Johann again, could this mad scheme succeed? What can a few unarmed men do against disciplined troops? How could Ziggner be sure of the hundreds of fellow conspirators of which he boasted?

Now Ziggner was pleading directly with him, the old friendly tone in his voice. "What do you think? Are you for it? Are you with us? Or maybe you'd rather be buried in a tattered uniform God knows where?"

Johann's mind raced desperately as all of them moved closer, the better to hear his answer. How could he let Ziggner down? Or the others, if they were agreed this was the thing to do? But how could it succeed? If he failed to agree, what might they do to him? He stared intently at the ring of faces above him. Every one of them betrayed the eagerness with which they awaited his answer.

"Well?" Ziggner's flat voice broke in on his spinning thoughts. The deep-lined face, jaw set, was hovering over him, shadowy in the flickering light.

Johann leaned back and slowly began to remove the other boot.

"You can count me in with you," he said, hoping he had been able to hide the tremor in his voice.

6

A PLOT'S FAILURE

THE days now passed with headlong speed as preparations continued for breaking camp, the down-river trip, embarkation to England, then to sea for America. When Johann wasn't relaying orders around the camp, he was busy helping check the supplies that rolled endlessly through the big gate.

Meanwhile, neither at the hut nor at headquarters did he hear any more about the plan to revolt and flee the camp. Indeed, his hut mates, having once divulged the plot to him, said little, apparently afraid he might change his mind and reveal everything to his superiors.

The night before the scheduled uprising, as Johann came near the hut, a dark figure rose from the shadows and approached him.

"Hsst! Is that you, Johann?" came a familiar voice.

Before he could reply, Baum was at Johann's side, steering him away from the hut with a solid grip on his arm.

"What's up, Baum? Why do you keep me from the hut?" asked Johann.

"Not so loud," grated Baum. "I've been tryin' to talk to you for days. Servin' as an aide, an' knowin' about this scatterbrained plan, I can understand how mixed up you must be these days. But I just wanted to warn you to have nothin' to do with it. Take my word, no good will come of it. Remember what I'm tellin' you. Stay clear of it." And before Johann could say a word, Baum was gone in the darkness.

The next morning when Johann woke, Ziggner, sleeping next to him, opened his eyes at about the same time. Looking cautiously about, he rose on one elbow and whispered, "Remember, it's tonight. At eight o'clock. Meet me here at seven thirty." Then Ziggner arose and dressed as did the others. No one else said anything.

The morning dragged by. Johann was busy checking the ammunition being brought into the camp and stored against the time of embarkation. With half a mind on his work he glanced up from time to time to look about the camp.

Nothing seemed out of the ordinary. Men were still

drilling and marching about the parade ground. The rat-tat-tat of the drum, the squeal of the fife came plainly to him. The clouds of dust sent up by the marching men rose to be blown away by a warm spring breeze. The sun twinkled on the brass fronts of the men's helmets as they wheeled and turned, obeying the shouted orders.

Suddenly, a rapid movement caught Johann's eye. Two lieutenants went by on the double, their swords clanking as they ran, a scared look on their faces. Johann saw them run directly to General von Kohrn's quarters, brush past the sentry, and go inside.

"How many boxes of ball did you put down, Leonhardt?" asked the sergeant in charge of the ammunition wagon working crew. Loath to take his eyes away from the General's door, Johann glanced quickly at the tally and replied, "Four dozen, sir."

But even as he looked, he heard a bugle sound. In a second, the scene before him changed. The men working beside the wagon dropped their loads, and, as the surprised sergeant cursed at them, formed a ring around the wagon.

Johann could see the bugler now, standing in front of the General's quarters. All around the enclosure men were running, hastily forming themselves up.

"Ta-ta-ta-ta!" came the bugle's notes again in the call to assemble. What had happened? As Johann ran toward headquarters, the General himself came out, surrounded by members of his staff. For a moment his huge bulk blocked the door. Johann ran up and saluted.

47

"Any orders for me, sir?" he asked.

Unnoticing, the General's little eyes stared across the space between buildings toward the gate. Johann followed his look to see the gates swinging shut. It was only eleven o'clock. What could this mean? A subordinate appeared, saluted, and announced, "Ranks ready and formed, sir."

Johann fell in behind the General and his staff as they moved slowly to the parade ground. Now an intense silence replaced the customary bustle. From somewhere outside the walls, Johann heard a cow lowing. The crows were chattering in the trees beyond the drill field. In front of Johann bobbed the shadows of the group, the General's one vast blot on the ground.

Now Johann saw the massed ranks of the regiment: row on row of burnished helmet fronts; file on file of blue and white uniforms; slant and slant of guns, their butts beside line on line of polished boots. Towering over his officers, the General turned to look once more at the gate. Then he faced forward. Still he stood silent. Then came a command:

"Present, arms!"

A thousand gleams of light flashed as the guns came to position with a cadenced jingle that sent shivers down Johann's spine.

"Salute, arms!"

A thousand blue-clad sleeves whipped to the salute and down again with a precision that spoke well for the military lessons of the weeks past.

"Order, arms!"

And, with a crunch that echoed from the camp walls

and sent the crows scattering, the butts came to earth.

At a nod from an aide, the bugler stepped forward and blew a fanfare. Backward he stepped—and forward strode the General.

"Men of the regiment," he began. Johann marveled at the carrying quality of that voice now. "Today is a sad one for our country. It has been brought to my attention that some of you plan to desert your country's— your Landgrave's service."

An astonished whisper ran through the massed ranks. It still sounded from the rear as the General continued:

"You men know it is a privilege to serve the Landgrave. He has pledged that service to His Majesty, the King of Great Britain. We must not fail that pledge. It is not for us to question his will. You are soldiers, and as soldiers you must bear your parts, willingly and cheerfully—without question.

"The names of those who have planned this scheme, unworthy of the name of Hessian, are known. Those who knew of the plan but took no part in it must inform on those who now do not willingly reveal their cowardice. It is your duty. Remember, we fight for the Landgrave. We cannot fail him."

The General paused, angrily flipped down the lace the wind had blown up about his face, then said:

"The squad leaders will step forward to receive the lists of the known traitors."

From front to rear, men bustled forward. Ramrod stiff, they took the papers from an aide, saluted, and returned to their places.

"Now," ordered the General, "you will call the

49

names of the men on your lists and order them to step a pace backward from their places in the ranks."

Almost unbelieving, Johann stood listening while the parade ground area sounded with the calling of names. In the ranks nearest him, man after man, answering the dread roll call, moved rearward, while their fellows, eyes still front, shifted uneasily as if to avoid any contact with the guilty. At last the calls ceased, the leaders came up to surrender their lists, saluted, then announced:

"Ranks in order, sir."

The bugler blew another call, "Close ranks." The long blue and white lines began shuffling together, closing up the vacant spaces that gaped in almost every row.

"Right, turn!" shouted the General's aide. With the clomping of a thousand boots, a twist of blue and white, the serried ranks obeyed.

"Forward, march!" The men began filing off, arms and legs swinging in cadence. "Halt!" came the command when they had gone a brief distance. Then, "Left, turn!" and once more the long ranks faced forward. The scattered files of the mutineers still stood in their original positions.

"Captain Weiderman, you will take charge of these men," ordered the General. "Secure them in the easternmost buildings. Put a twenty-four-hour guard over them and see that none escape until it is decided what punishment they will receive." To the tap-tap-tap of a single drum, the mutineers were marched from the parade ground, their stacked guns remaining mutely behind them.

The bugle sounded the "Dismiss" and the rest of the regiment moved slowly away, a vast buzzing rising all around as they went. The plot had been foiled. But how?

By late afternoon, the number of mutineers whose names had been called was known. More than five hundred were involved. Many more, who might yet be informed on, might be added to the list. What would happen to them was the thought uppermost in everyone's mind. But Johann thought, will I be blamed by Ziggner and the others for the plan's failure?

7

A VOYAGE

SEVERAL weeks later as he lay in the stifling, crowded hold of the troop transport on which he and the others had embarked at Bremerlehe, Johann wished the mutiny had succeeded.

With his fellow Hessians—few of whom had ever seen the sea, let alone sailed on it—Johann quickly found that transports were built for one purpose—to get as many men as possible from one place to another, with time no object, comfort the least of concerns.

As he watched the swinging ship's lantern cast its

dim ray around the deck, Johann felt a stabbing ache in his right side. If he could only roll over! How he wished he could! But jammed tight against him was Kampel's broad back. Immediately behind him lay "Father" Claus. Beyond them in turn, facing the same way, lay Gorthalman, Baum, and Ziggner. All were snoring loudly.

Baum, old soldier that he was, had taken the best position, his back against the next bulkhead. He, at least, had some freedom of movement, not an inconsiderable thing when, according to the transport rules, the men had to sleep "spoon" fashion.

It was Baum who had explained it the first night after the coast of England had dropped out of sight behind a tossing waste of crested green waves.

"This ain't goin' to be any down-river trip," he'd said, referring to the barge trip to Bremerlehe. That had been cold enough, lying in open boats, trying to get some sleep.

"We're likely to be on this tub for five, six, or maybe seven weeks," he said. "If each of us was to have a nice comfortable place for himself, they'd need half a dozen transports."

Ziggner cut in, "All right, so we all know you've served before. What are you tryin' to tell us?"

"Just this. We'll all have to sleep in this space here, tight, close to one another. An' I hope nobody gets no nightmares. When somebody gets tired sleepin' on one side, he'll have to tell the fellow next him an' so on, till we've all turned over. It's called 'spoon' fashion. Get it?"

Johann had looked at the little area sandwiched in between two stanchions, and wondered how six men were to sleep in the space. The narrow, low-ceilinged compartment had seemed dark and had smelled horribly of sea water then. Now, as he lay sleepless, it smelled even worse.

Unable to bear the pain any longer, Johann poked "Father" Claus. He was easier to wake than Kampel, a heavy sleeper. "Shift, Claus, shift," he whispered. The monk's regular snores kept on. Johann could feel his breath against his neck, the bony knees ramming into his own thighs.

"Wha-what's that?" Father Claus murmured drowsily.

"Move," whispered Johann again. "My right side's killing me."

Grunting, Claus passed the word along to the man behind him, Johann at the same time nudging Kampel half awake. Then, with a concert of protests and groans, the six shifted in unison. Johann sighed with relief. He no longer had to watch the light bobbing and turning with the motion of the transport.

But now he had a new difficulty. Kampel, stouter than "Father" Claus, was taking up more than his share of space. Try as he would, sleep wouldn't come.

A hundred images of the weeks that had passed since the discovery of the mutiny now came to his wakeful brain. It was he who had been called on to compile the lists of the mutineers. He had been shaken to find that of his hut mates only Claus and Baum had escaped being named as conspirators.

Gorthalman, old as he was, and another had been sentenced to be hanged, and thirty had been ordered to run the gantlet as an example to the rest of the mutineers.

"Ach," General von Kohrn had said, "we've already put the embarkation off a day. And we can't hang them all. If we do, how is the Landgrave to get his money? Better to have a few set an example for the rest. Let them run the gantlet tomorrow at eleven o'clock. The other two we'll hang at noon."

The running of the gantlet was all that Baum had told Johann it would be. Stripped to the waist and lined up, one behind the other, the thirty had been forced to run between a double line of fifty soldiers facing each other, their long bayonet belts in their hands.

At a signal, the men, fear written on each face, began their desperate race down between the long rows of their loyal fellows. As they passed, the heavy belts swished through the air. "Thwack! Thwack!" the long belts slashed at the cringing white bodies. Some staggered and fell, but it didn't help them. Under the rules they had to finish the course on the run. So they rose to lurch onward to the end.

At the end of the line, though, stood surgeon's aides, ready to apply unguents to the bruised and bleeding bodies. The running had been carried out in full view of the regiment, the rest of the mutineers placed right behind the double rows to watch the ordeal. As he watched it, Johann had been conscious of a pair of eyes boring through him and, turning once, saw Ziggner, who was not among the thirty, looking in his direction.

When Johann had half smiled at him, the other dropped his gaze and shifted his eyes to the scene before him. Gorthalman and the other condemned man had been brought out then and marched toward the gallows set up on the parade ground. But as they stood, nooses about their necks, the hanging had been canceled on the General's orders. The old man had been more dead than alive when he was led away.

The next day they were all marched several miles to the river and put aboard barges for the trip to Bremerlehe, the late mutineers included. Johann had been fearful of what his former hut mates might say. He was afraid they might believe it was he who betrayed the plot. But he was surprised to find that none of them mentioned it. Gorthalman and Kampel marched stolidly along. Only Ziggner seemed different. When the others joined in the general conversation, Ziggner kept to himself. Johann thought he avoided talking directly to him. When he spoke of this to Baum, the veteran replied:

"Ain't you the simple one. They know when they're well off. Myself, I think Ziggner spilled it for all he seemed so anxious. Now, I think, he wants to make 'em feel you had somethin' to do with it. But don't forget, the officers know a lad in irons ain't paid for by the British."

There had been jeers and cheers for them when they reached Bremerlehe as they clumped from the barges to the transport, the first seagoing ship Johann had ever seen. But they'd hardly progressed two miles into the North Sea when half of them became seasick. Even the brief halt in England, at Portsmouth, for their final inspection and loading of stores, hadn't helped much. They were sick all over again when they got out on the Atlantic.

By that time it was much better to stay on deck as long as possible, in spite of the cold wind. For the holds below were thick with retching, groaning men.

His mind whirling with these thoughts, Johann finally fell asleep for all of Kampel's snores right in his ear. He had hardly done so, it seemed, when the bugle awoke him. All around men began to wake, to curse, to yawn. Then slowly—unless prodded by a squad leader's boot—they rose, stretched, glad to be free of the miserable "spoon" beds.

"Well, what do you suppose we'll have for breakfast this mornin'?" asked Ziggner, trying to button his uniform while struggling to stand erect against the transport's motion. A faint beam of sunlight straggled down the hatchway, dancing here and there on a gun barrel, on a tarnished helmet front. Gradually, the ship came awake for another day.

"What's the use of asking that?" grunted Claus. "It's always the same thing. Either pork and pease—or pease and pork."

"That's what we had yesterday, an' the day afore that, aye, an' the day afore that, too," growled Kampel. He dabbed at his eyes with his cuff as he added, "Ho, when I think of those dumplin's my mother used to make. . . ." He stopped, then added, "But today, now, why maybe we'll be lucky. Maybe we'll have salt beef and pease."

Baum, always the first dressed, watched the grimy, sleep-heavy men flounder into their clothes. "What's the use of kickin'?" he rasped. "You'll get used to it. In another month, that is."

Johann shivered as he heard this. Another month? If the first weeks were like this—how would anybody stand another four?

"You know what, Baum?" said Ziggner. "I heard on deck the other day they keep the ship's crew busy nights, with cannon balls breakin' up that ship's biscuit they give us. That's so's we can eat it."

"Wouldn't surprise me none," replied Baum. "One o' the crew was tellin' me t'other day this biscuit was the same the Britishers laid in for the French and Indian Wars."

"You mean the one they called the Seven Years' War?" asked Kampel. "Why that was twenty years ago!"

"I don't mean no other," replied Baum. "They say its been in Portsmouth, where we stopped, ever since then. They wanted to get rid o' it, so's they gave it to us!"

The long days at sea passed with few changes in the routine. Each morning muster was held on deck. Then at noon the miserable portion of food was doled out, each man fighting with the others to get a place with a back rest to sit while forcing the stuff down.

When the weather permitted, daily drill was held. Then the same moldy food for dinner, perhaps washed down with a draft of warm beer. The afternoons, Johann found, dragged the worst. Pitching and rolling up and down endless green waves that moved steadily from the west, the transport labored up one watery mountain, slid down the other side—and then did it all over again.

Evenings came early, but Johann preferred to stay on deck till the stars came out and the wind whistled through the rigging with a dismal, wailing sound. As he stood in the fading light, Johann wondered for the hundredth time what would happen when he and the rest landed in the New World? What would it be like to fire his gun at a live target—at another human? Was this America as wild as they said?

The ship's bell struck eight times. Time to turn in. If he waited any longer he'd have trouble getting into the crowded cubicle below. Slowly, holding on to the bulwark, he moved toward the mainmast where others were already gathered for a last drink before retiring. When it came his turn, he dipped the scummy, greasy water from the barrel, held his nose, and took a quick gulp. Its taste was fearful, but it was the only water they had.

Johann hated to leave the tossing, but clean-aired sea for the hold. And again the thought struck him: how would he meet Herr Crainter; how get possession of his father's watch? He took a last, long look at the winking stars and ducked down the hatch.

8

A NEW COUNTRY

THE weather turned warmer as June gave way to July.
For days at a time the lumbering transport was be-
calmed and lay rolling in the sea. Now to seasickness was
added the toll taken by poor food. One-third of the men
aboard, Johann included, fell victim to illness.

He was seated by the bulwark one day, trying to take
advantage of the scant shade it afforded, when he felt a
spinning sensation in his head. Black spots appeared before his eyes. He tried to rise, gripping the rough wood
of the bulwark. Then he fell back, unconscious.

60

When he opened his eyes again he found himself on a pallet in the hold. His body burned with fever; his head pounded as though it would burst.

"Here, lad," someone said. "Open your mouth and take this." Dimly, he saw a man, a surgeon's aide, standing beside him, bottle in hand. Johann obediently gulped the liquid, but almost at once sat up to spit out the burning, acrid draft.

"What is it?" he choked.

"Just something that'll make you better," cheerfully replied the man. "You've your first touch of the sickness. But it won't be the last. So drink up again." And he offered the bottle again. The taste of the medicine nearly gagged Johann. He lay back and lost consciousness once more.

When he roused, Johann was first aware of the groans and murmurs of others in the surgeon's cubicle. Then, as his head cleared, he distinguished voices nearer to him. They came to him faintly for a few seconds; then, when he comprehended what was being said, he forgot his aches and fever.

"I tell you," the first voice said, "this has gone on long enough. We'll be at sea until we've long gray beards. Me, I don't intend to rot on this tub an' then—maybe if we ever get off it—be shot at by some fool farmer. I'm goin' to do somethin' about it."

A second voice replied, "But what can you do?"

"Well, this is what I've thought out," replied the other man. "You know the pill roller only goes through here once an hour. I've managed to get a bit o' flint an' a steel. All I have to do is strike them, set fire to one o' these rotten blankets—an' it's done."

"Done?" queried the second man. "How?"

"You an' me will crawl aft soon's it's set. When it gets a good hold, we'll sound the alarm. 'Tis simple. The hulk will be burned badly enough to halt the journey, damaged so's they'll have to turn around an' go back. Now, do you get it?"

"But what about these other fellows in here?" asked the second man.

"Them." The voice was scornful. "They don't even know whether they're alive or dead. They can't be any worse off."

Despite his fever, Johann shivered as he heard the words. The prospect of having to toss all the way back to Portsmouth, where they'd been checked and approved for the payment to the Landgrave by the British King's inspector, Colonel Fawcitt, made Johann tremble.

He tried to rise but could not. His head hammered again; his blood throbbed in his ears. But as he lay there, weak and perspiring, the little cubicle suddenly became brighter with a flickering light!

Turning, Johann saw someone, not ten feet away, kneeling and striking flint and steel. As he watched, helpless, the sparks showered down. A second tiny flame glowed, illuminating the face above. It was Ziggner!

Johann rolled over and, summoning every reserve of strength, staggered to his feet, head pounding, ears ringing.

"Ziggner!" he heard himself croak. "Stop! For the love of heaven, stop!"

Surprised, Ziggner looked up from his work, hesitated a moment, then struck flint and steel together again.

Johann tried one swaying step closer.

"Ziggner, listen!" he pleaded. "Have you no care for the rest of these fellows here? Remember, you said once we were all in this together?"

There was no answer from the other, now striking furiously.

"I know you think I betrayed the plot to mutiny. But I didn't. I was willing to go along with you. I said so, didn't I? But even if you don't believe me, think of the rest of these lads. Think, Ziggner, think—and stop!"

Around Johann the others began to stir now. Some, faces set and pale, gazed wonderingly at the flame. Others were trying to struggle to their feet.

For the first time Ziggner answered Johann.

"Leonhardt, I've done all my thinkin'. 'Specially about you, you pen-pushin' clerk. An' me thinkin' I had a friend! Ha! We're in it together, eh? You mean you're in it—for Leonhardt! Well, you bilked me last time, but this time, you're too late!"

In the next minute, Ziggner reached down, scooped up the now flaming blanket, and flung it toward the bulkhead. Then his intention became clear to Johann. At that side lay a pile of blankets! Almost instantly one caught fire, then another! The hold began to fill with a dense choking smoke, made lurid by the rising flames!

Ziggner began backing away, and as he did, his words

63

told Johann too plainly that the earlier friendship had been replaced by a violent hatred.

"You can't do nothin' this time, you milksop!" he yelled. " 'Fore you can tell the General this time, you'll be done for! You've turned on your friends for the last time, Johann Leonhardt—an' 'twill be a bitter lesson to you. You'll know now, maybe, that a man can't lightly turn aside the friendship of Adolph Ziggner!"

Ziggner backed nearer the hatch. "Those blankets are just as shoddy as those shoes we took out of that case three weeks ago! New boots, they said they was! An' what did they turn out to be? A bunch of blinkin' ladies slippers! Slippers! Ha, ha, ha!" His voice echoed through the smoke. "Slippers for the Landgrave's soldiers!"

Now he was at the ladder leading to the hatch. Behind him, staggering, crawling, crying, tears streaming down their faces, the rest of the sick tried to follow. But the first few fell, and in a minute a mass of writhing arms and legs, bodies and heads, piled up at the foot of the ladder!

Tottering toward the now fiercely blazing heap, Johann shielded his eyes against the heat, then began to kick at the pile. Flames seared his arms and legs, smoke choked him, but he kept at it. Then, in a brighter flash, he saw the outlines of a closed port! It was a minute's work to fling it open!

The cool sea air poured through the port, fanning the flames higher. But Johann now worked with desperate frenzy. One, two, then three blazing blankets went out the port! From behind him he heard shouts and orders. In the next minute he was joined by sailors with buckets of water and stout poles. Some poured water on the flames; others poked the rest of the blankets through the port. At last the fire was out!

Two weeks later, when Johann had almost recovered from his burns, he was summoned to the great cabin amidships. Ranged along the table were General von Kohrn and the principal officers of the regiment. Johann stiffly raised an arm in salute.

"So this is the lad who saved the ship, eh, Colonel?" asked the General. Then, after a longer look at the wondering Johann, he exclaimed:

"*Donner!* It's the same one who served me in the encampment." He paused, looked quickly around, then added, "How do you feel, boy?"

"Better now, sir," replied Johann.

"Well, I've got something that should make you mend even faster," said the General. "Step up here, lad."

Reaching into a drawer before him, the General pulled out a chevron—a corporal's chevron!

"Because of your efforts in saving our ship and the lives of His Highness's men, Johann Leonhardt, you are hereby promoted to the rank of corporal." He reached forward to grasp Johann's still bandaged right hand in his own big hand, but almost as quickly, while the other officers stared, withdrew it, and said:

"Corporal, you may retire."

Kampel and Claus were waiting outside. Their eyes widened when they saw the chevron.

"So," laughed Claus, "now we'll have to take our

orders from this whippersnapper, eh, Kampel?" But Kampel said nothing. He just patted Johann's shoulder.

The next day the notice of the promotion was posted, together with a more somber one. The second noted that Ziggner had been found guilty by a court-martial of attempting to "destroy his Highness's vessel on the high seas, with intent thereby to cause the deaths of his fellow soldiers." Ziggner, it said, would be confined to the ship's brig, or jail, until landing in America. Then he would be executed in accordance with military law.

But Ziggner's impending fate was forgotten when, a few days later, all on deck heard a hail from the lookout:

"Sails, ho!"

Every man ran to line the bulwarks, for up to that time the transport had sighted no other ship at all.

"Where away?" cried the ship's captain. "Can you make out how many?"

"Sou' by sou'west," came the reply. "Looks like twenty-five or thirty of 'em."

An orderly hurried below to tell the General, who, with his officers, joined the hundreds on deck, all craning their necks in the direction indicated by the lookout.

For several minutes Johann could see nothing. All at once, a flash of white caught his eye. Then another, and another. Slowly, majestically, first the sails, then the hulls of a fleet appeared.

As he watched, a puff of smoke floated upward from the largest of the ships. In its wake the bows of the

66

others rhythmically dipped and rose in the green sea. Then he heard a distant boom.

With a creaking of blocks and slapping of the huge sails, the transport changed course and made for the flotilla. At the same time the roar of a cannon aboard her deafened Johann and his fellows. It was the first time they'd heard a gun at sea. From the direction of the bridge, a bugle blew the assembly call.

"Must be something big up," said Kampel. "They can't be enemy ships. We wouldn't be standing toward them."

When the ranks were formed, General von Kohrn mounted to the bridge, speaking trumpet in hand. The bugle blew for silence, and he began:

"Men of the regiment, you have proved you are ready to meet all risks and dangers for the Landgrave. The fleet you've seen will assure you that we are not alone in our fight. For, besides the British warships, you'll see there are several other transports with other brave men like yourselves aboard. They have had a quicker passage than we did. We are going to join the fleet, and I may tell you now that we are about two day's sail from our destination, New York. That is all. Dismiss!"

An excited buzz broke out all about the deck. Was it really true, thought Johann, that the long, tedious voyage would soon be over, and once more he'd see land, real land? That he would reach New York, find Herr Crainter, and get the watch at last?

Baum's voice broke in on his thoughts. "Well, lads," he said cheerfully, "what did I tell you? We're goin' to

67

make it, an' in good company too. Then ho, for those fat pickin's in America, eh?"

There were few who remained below decks during the next two days. Everyone able to stand lined the bulwarks, peering westward as the fleet, paced by the tall men-o'-war, bright in their fresh paint, pressed on. Johann, as eager as the others for the first sight of land, was watching, too, when he felt a tap on his shoulder.

"You're to report to the cabin at once," the orderly told him.

This time he found the General alone in the cabin.

"Corporal," began the General, "I've a message to send over to Colonel von Donop on the transport *Zweiger*. I want you to order a boat and take it to him at once."

Soon Johann found himself pitching wildly in a small boat, the distance between his own transport and the *Zweiger* rapidly narrowing under the strong and skillful oarsmanship of two seamen. Then he was below the sheer side of the other ship, the waves threatening to dash the little craft against the gray-green, dripping hull. A rope was thrown down, and while the sailors fended off the boat, Johann was hauled aboard.

"Messenger from General von Kohrn reporting to Colonel von Donop," he said.

The officer on duty led him below, and he found himself face to face with a colonel in the grenadiers. He saluted and handed his message to the officer, a short, gray-haired man, then retired to await his answer.

Johann was surrounded by half a dozen troopers when he emerged. All were anxious for any news he might give them of his voyage, or of the men aboard. He was trying to answer their questions when a hail came from above:

"Land, ho!"

A mighty cheer arose all around. With the others, Johann ran to stare. It was no mistake. There it was, a flat, sandy bit of land rising above the sea, topped by rolling green hills. Nearer Johann saw hundreds of ships, their masts and spars like a water-borne forest, riding at anchor in a broad bay! As he looked, puffs of smoke appeared above every ship. And the swelling roar of hundreds of cannon sounded over the sea, sparkling now in the August sun. The long voyage had ended at last, thought Johann! This was America!

AN OMEN

THE long, curving piece of land off which the ships were anchored was called Staten Island, Johann learned, as he made the return trip to his own transport. Off to the right in the summer's haze he could see another long stretch of coast line. That, said one of the sailors, was Long Island, a prosperous farming area.

"But where is New York?" asked Johann. "I thought we were landing there."

"It'll take a bit of doing to reach that, lad," the sailor

laughed. "Some of these ships you see have been here in the Lower Bay as it's called since early June."

He then pointed out the watery gap that separated Long Island and Staten Island. "Them's the Narrows," he said. "The ships will have to go through there before they can reach the Upper Bay an' New York. An' they tell me the rebels are entrenched at the other side of Long Island, batteries of cannon an' all. 'Twon't be easy."

The next day while taking in the busy water-front scene—the boats plying between ship and ship, or between ship and shore, listening to the rolling drums from the Staten Island shore where he saw the red-coated British troops drilling—Baum suddenly shouted:

"Look! Out to sea! There's more ships a-comin' in! Look!"

It was true. Johann counted nearly a hundred sail as they rose above the horizon and moved toward the anchorage.

"Must be the biggest fleet that was ever assembled anywhere," grated Baum. "Where are they goin' to anchor, now?"

Baum gazed a moment longer, then said:

"You know, if'n they get any more we'll be able to walk dry-footed across decks to land."

The air clattered and crackled as hundreds of guns boomed a welcoming salute, and re-echoed again as the new flotilla answered. Now Johann estimated that more than three hundred ships and transports and close to half a hundred warships were anchored about. The commotion grew greater as the new fleet neared. Spars rattled and blocks creaked; uncounted waterspouts appeared as anchors were dropped. Almost instantly, the boats, always the little boats, crawled from one ship to another, or with oars flashing in the sun, moved toward the shore.

The next day Johann and his fellow Hessians were ordered into a fleet of barges and transported to the hard-trodden beaches. It felt good to walk once more on dry land, hard as that seemed after months aboard a moving ship.

The regiment lined up, and with a drummer tapping out the beat, marched smartly up a winding road to the encampment on the heights above the shore. It was hot work toiling through the sandy soil, Johann found, hotter than he had ever experienced in his life. Under his heavy uniform the sweat coursed down his back and chest. He wondered if America was always as hot.

The encampment was a maze of rude huts, tents, and ammunition trains. When the regiment reached it, they were greeted by the applauding shouts of the Hessian contingents previously landed from the other ships, and by the catcalls of the Britishers. But out of the mass of howling, shouting men an aide appeared and directed them to their sector of the encampment.

The voices of the thousands around him dazed Johann. The smoke from smoldering campfires almost blotted out the sun. Helpful hands soon raised the tents or threw together rude brush huts. Eager questions and answers flew about as the earlier arrivals showered the newcomers with comment and advice.

It was from them Johann learned that the British,

whose red coats far outnumbered the blue of the Hessians or the green of the Jägers, had landed on July 5, more than a month before. The first weeks on the island had been miserable, with most men required to sleep in thin blankets, practically on the seashore. They had been plagued at night by an insect not known in Europe, the mosquito. Its bites and stinging had not endeared the country to the British soldiers.

"But where are the rebels?" asked Johann of one man. "Has there been any fighting yet?"

"Only among ourselves—and with the tongue, mostly," he replied. "The rebels came to New York in force earlier this year after their army forced the British to leave Boston town in Massachusetts last March. They've occupied New York. It's on the south end of a long island you can't see from here in this haze. It's girded on the west by the North River—some call it Hudson's River—and on the east by the East River. Right now, they have a fort this side of the East River on a height called Brooklyn. But we ain't seen any of them yet."

The heat continued unbroken by a single shower. There had been no rain, Johann learned, for three weeks. And yet there had been no move to start any action against the rebel forces. Everyone, he found, wondered what the British commander in chief, Sir William Howe, intended to do.

"Ach," said Colonel von Donop to the General one day in Johann's hearing, "these British. There's no telling what they'll do. Maybe they like to fight in the rain better."

73

The General, mopping his sweating brow, had replied, "It's a mad business anyway. Why, will you tell me, with all these farms and fine houses should anyone want to revolt against their king? In my opinion, it's laziness and too much good living that made them dissatisfied." He paused, then added, "And yet General Howe and his brother, the Admiral of the fleet, are still trying to pacify them."

"Aye," replied the little colonel. "Meanwhile nearly twenty thousand men sit here in this hole and sweat themselves away. I don't understand them."

The criticism against Sir William disappeared a week later, however, when word was given that the men were to be re-embarked on the transports. The story about the camp was that British warships had already passed rebel batteries and barriers along the North River, that aside from a part of the colonist army on Brooklyn, the rest was all but bottled up in New York.

Baum was indignant when he heard of the order. But his anger lasted only a minute, and he said, "Well, at least we won't have to suffer this heat an' these insects much longer. Looks to me like one good fight an' we'll have 'em. We'll all be back in the old country by Christmas with our pockets jinglin'."

There was yet another reason Baum was not sorry to leave Staten Island. The rebel natives, Johann and the others soon found, had fled carrying fowl and flocks with them. The army was forced to subsist largely on its own rations brought in the ships. "Ach," moaned Baum, "if I could only get my hands on a nice fat sheep."

The night before the embarkation, the sun set in an

angry red glare hardly noticed by the busy soldiers preparing for the next morning's start. Claus, Kampel, and Gorthalman were standing beside their tent when Baum came strolling up.

"You fellows want to have some fun?" he asked.

"What's up?" asked Kampel. "If it's anything that'll mean a walk, I'm against it. This heat is beginning to be more than I can bear."

"Come on," Baum invited. "Come with me. It ain't far."

With Kampel still protesting, the three followed Baum down the company "street," then on toward the parade ground. From all sides of the camp now, men were moving to the same spot, talking, pushing, cursing the heat and the insects.

"What's goin' to happen?" asked Gorthalman.

"You'll see," Baum said mysteriously.

They soon found themselves part of a throng that made a circle about a cleared space on the parade ground. In this space was piled high a batch of wood, barrels, and other waste material. Then it was that Kampel caught sight of four lifelike figures perched atop the heap.

"I see it," he commented to the others. "They're going to burn somebody in effigy. Who're they supposed to be, Baum?"

"Hanged if I know," muttered Baum, watching the lighted torches being applied to the pile. He turned to the man next to him and asked a question. Then he turned back.

"Fellow here says one of them is supposed to repre-

75

sent this farmer rebel general, Washington. Doesn't know who the others are."

In the dusk, the red tongues of flame began to lick at the heap. The smoke rose into the air, big billowing clouds of it, almost as large as those that now were blowing up in the western sky. Higher and higher they mounted, the ruddy reflection lighting thousands of faces standing or seated around the blazing pile.

A roar arose from the crowd as the first effigy's lower parts caught fire and began to crackle fiercely. Bright yellow flames shot up, illuminating the grotesque, painted features. With a yet bigger blob of flame the entire figure was consumed. An approving shout went up all around.

"Must have 'em coated with pitch," observed Baum. "They sure make a fine glow."

Quickly, the second caught and went up to the sound of another cheer. The third was just beginning to catch, when an even brighter light came from behind—this time from the heavens. A jagged streak of lightning tore through the clouds. The answering boom of the thunder followed almost at once. And, as though making way for its arrival, the wind suddenly whipped up at the same time.

Now the crimson glow of the bonfire conflicted for a few minutes with the dazzling light from the skies. But only for a moment, for, with a mighty sighing sound, wind-driven rain sheeted down. Stunned by the sound of the thunderclaps, gasping as the rain slashed savagely at them, Johann and the others in the crowd began to leave. At first it seemed good to feel the cooling rain, but in minutes Johann was soaking wet and running, pushing, and hurrying back to his tent, the way lighted by the incessant glare of lightning. Behind, the bonfire smoldered and steamed in the rain.

Shivering, the four huddled in their tent, gripping for dear life at its frail edges as the wind raged and tore at it with increasing fury. Outside, the skies were torn and torn again with lightning, while the thunderclaps fairly shook the ground. Johann had never before experienced such a storm.

"So this is the New World," chattered Claus. "One minute I'm roasting, the next I'm half frozen and soaked."

Something struck the side of the tent, bulged it, then moved around to the entrance. A soldier reeled in, water streaming down his face, his shoes squishing with every step. In the next flash, Johann caught a glimpse of his face. The eyes were wide, the face drawn.

"What happened?" yelled Baum above the roar.

The man appeared not to have heard the question.

"It's only a thunderstorm, soldier," rasped Baum. "Get over here out of that rip in the roof or you'll never dry out. Tell me, what happened?"

The strange soldier stared at them again, but Johann thought he didn't really see them.

"What's the matter, man?" he asked.

"Those effigies," he mumbled, his words almost lost in the noise outside. "Oh, those effigies. They all went up in smoke—save one."

"An' whose was that?" asked Baum.

"The—the one o' the rebel general," muttered the soldier. And he crossed himself as he said it.

A louder crash than any yet heard followed his statement. No one spoke, but they all listened to the rain slashing away at the canvas roof above them. It was Kampel who spoke first.

"And," his voice seemed to hesitate, "why was that?"

The staring eyes seemed unblinking even in the next flash.

"I don't know. Nobody knows. Maybe 'tis an omen," he said.

Long after midnight the storm blew itself out. Soaked as they were, all turned in, for the orders were for a dawn embarkation on the transports.

Johann, who had many times in the past few weeks wished he could be cool again, shivered in his blanket. For a long time sleep did not come. Tomorrow, he thought, we may go into battle with the rebels. What would happen? Could it be true what the sheltering soldier had said? Was the refusal of the enemy general's effigy to burn really an omen?

10

A FIRST BATTLE

A HOT sun blazed in the cloudless sky as Johann looked up the long dusty Flatbush Road. Starting in the flat lands over which his battalion had advanced from their landing place at Gravesend Bay, it wound on and up to the wooded ridge he could just make out, about three miles distant.

As far to his left and right as he could see, long, orderly ranks of men were standing quietly, all eyes on the road. It was already toward noon, but as yet there had been no sign of any active engagement in Johann's sector, the honored center of the royal army.

Already, Johann had undergone his first fire. The day the Hessians had landed on Long Island, a detachment of rebels had appeared outside the little village of Flatbush, exchanged a few shots, and retreated.

He had hardly comprehended that first foe he met outside the village, now behind the massed army. Just for a fleeting moment he had seen a poorly clad man standing before him; seen his musket barrel glint in the sunlight, then a puff of smoke. It wasn't until the vicious zing of the bullet sped past his head that he'd realized he'd been the target. His knees had shaken, his hands trembled when he found another fellow human had fired at him.

Before he could trigger his own weapon, the shirt-sleeved enemy disappeared. Johann had seen his own shot harmlessly shatter a twig on the bush, but that was all. His first exchange of shots, he found, was far different from those practice ones back home.

Unlike the Hessians, the rebels did not fire by volleys on command. Instead, they used the wiles of a hunter, lying singly behind trees, bushes, or stone walls, firing at long range usually, then retreating. Few of them, indeed, even wore distinctive uniforms, unless, perhaps, you excepted a cockade in an ordinary civilian hat.

To Johann it seemed all rebels must look like the natives who, when the Hessians first landed on Long Island, flocked into the camp, loudly proclaiming their loyalty. To prove it, they brought fresh vegetables and meat, the first the Hessians had seen for months. The men were tall and thin, talked in high, twanging voices; the women mostly neatly dressed and pretty.

But now, on this August day, the army was awaiting a signal. The road before it was one of four that climbed over the hills, where the rebels were reported to have some advance works, to the stronger fortification at Brooklyn. Beyond lay New York, on the far side of the East River.

There was no question that they were still there in those seemingly innocent woods. Every now and then a ball would come whistling over. But the shots were infrequent, largely, someone said, because the rebels had to conserve their little stores of powder.

What, Johann wondered for the tenth time, had happened to the British forces on the right under Lord Percy and General Clinton?

Hours before dawn they had started, bound for the Jamaica road and an unguarded pass through the hills. The route would take them around the rebel left flank, and they could fall on the foe from the rear. Had the surprise move, so carefully planned, failed?

Two hours ago, heavy skirmishing had been heard on the left where General Grant's British were trying to feint the rebels out of position along the Gowanus Road. But no news had yet come from that direction. An hour ago, Lieutenant General Philip von Heister, newly arrived head of all German forces in King George's army, had ordered a brisk cannonading, "to flush them out of the woods," as the order said.

The earth quivered as the batteries loosed one round after another, the sweating cannoneers serving their guns like very devils. Nothing had happened. Now only an occasional rebel shot could be heard.

Again Johann looked up the road. It was hard to believe that up there, somewhere, were other men, guns in hand, howitzers primed and ready, awaiting the Hessian advance. Men like those around him no doubt. Men with fathers and mothers, yes, even with children at home.

The fathers or grandfathers of these rebels had fled their own homes in Europe or England and set up in each of their colonies a government much different than that of, say, Hesse-Cassel. Every man, it was said, had something to say about how he was to be governed. And they'd become so used to their own style of government that they resented the King's attempts to dictate to them.

Many, though, were still anxious to remain within the British King's realm. Many were anxious to aid the British against their fellow Americans. Indeed, some of these had offered to guide Lord Percy's men around the rebel lines to a weakly guarded spot on the left.

Up until six weeks ago, Johann had found out, it was still a question whether the majority really wanted to separate from the mother country, England. Then the leaders of the rebellion had signed what they called a "Declaration of Independence" in Philadelphia, the rebels' chief town. Since that date, and despite the peacemaking efforts of the British commander in chief and his brother, Admiral Howe, feeling had hardened. Why, on the night the Declaration had been received in New York, only weeks ago, a mob had torn down a statue of the British King!

A horseman now clattered up the road from Flatbush, interrupting Johann's reverie. He cantered to the spot where General von Heister and his staff stood in the shade of a tree. He leaned down and handed over a dispatch. There was a stir among the officers as soon as the General opened it and read it. All mounted and rode forward until they were in front of the massed lines, General von Kohrn the nearest to Johann's battalion.

A bugle blew, the General raised his hat, and spoke: "Men of Hesse-Cassel, you are about to engage in battle with the army of those who have rebelled against their rightful sovereign. Our task is to take that ridge immediately ahead. We have been purposely given that honor. The rebels are entrenched, but are far fewer than we, and not nearly as well armed. At any moment now, our British allies on the right will engage them from the rear. You will take them in the front. They are trapped, and cannot escape our combined might. A cannon shot will signify that engagement. When you hear it, advance! Advance for God and Landgrave!"

Up and down the long lines men began raising and lowering their weapons to test their readiness, slid their bayonets from their sheaths to be sure they were handy, pulled at cartridge belts, tugged helmets on more firmly. A knot tied itself just then in the pit of Johann's stomach; his heart began to beat faster. What would it be like in the thick of battle? To see men fall? Perhaps to be wounded himself? He wondered. Did a ball hurt much when it pierced the flesh?

But now there was no more time for thinking. Far away through the sultry summer's air came a distant cannon's boom! The signal! The buglers blew fanfares

on their shining trumpets; hoarse commands sounded all along the lines; the blue-clad ranks, double file, began to march! Now the drums rolled out their foot-quickening tempo, the fifes began to squeal! The battle, at last, was about to be joined!

Johann marched a few paces in front of the foremost rank. Onward the men went, sunlight shining on barrel and helmet. His first feeling of unease left him when he turned briefly to see the sturdy rows behind him crunching forward. Nearest to him marched Kampel and Claus. Their usually pale faces were flushed with the day's heat. Sweat was rolling down Kampel's cheeks, dripping from his chin, staining his uniform collar.

Up ahead, somewhere, were von Donop's Jägers, former huntsmen, specially recruited for this duty in a wild country. The rebels disliked open combat, feared the bayonet it was said, and customarily used the fighting tactics of the savages they'd found when the country first was settled.

On marched the blue lines, step by step, yard by yard. There was no sign of the enemy, no firing from the heavily wooded crests in front. Then with shocking suddenness, came a crashing volley. Johann's impulse was to throw himself to the ground, to crawl out of reach of the singing missiles that snapped bits of twigs and small limbs from the trees overhead. But from the corner of his eye he saw the men behind him calmly moving on, and in a moment his panic passed. A cloud of white smoke drifted from the brush up ahead.

"Hold your fire," came the order. "Make them fire again. Their fire is too high! It can't harm you."

Now the ground began to rise rapidly, the trees to thicken; the bushes were heavier and closer together. It was hard work to keep a formation. Still no enemy showed himself. Then with a deadly snapping and patter of twigs and leaves, a second leaden shower struck. Johann heard a cry behind him and turned to see a man lying on the ground, clutching at his leg. It

85

was Gorthalman! Even as he looked, the gaps in the ranks were closed up and the line still moved forward, a grim, scared look on every set face.

"Do not fire!" The order was repeated up and down the ranks. Johann's weapon, carried at the ready for twenty minutes, weighed nearly a ton. But what was there to fire at? Somewhere off to his right, a bugle sounded a new signal. It was taken up and repeated, to the right, to the left.

"Fix bayonets!"

Came the sound of a thousand bayonets being drawn from sheaths; ten times a hundred whispers of sudden and violent combat. Came the clatter and rattle as the bayonets were jammed home in place; a thousand locks were snapped shut on unseen lives ahead.

Again the voice of the bugle.

"Charge, Hessians!"

The cadenced march turned into a frenzied thrashing of bush and wiry, tufted grass as the Hessians lunged forward as one man. Now, surely, the enemy must appear!

Then Johann saw it. A little mound of earth, almost hidden by the greenery. And just at its topmost edge, the mouth of a small howitzer. Behind it, some men in shirt sleeves were ramming home a charge. On the dead run, Johann made for it, trembling at every step as his eye fixed itself on that small brazen hole atop the parapet.

With a deafening roar it went off. Johann threw himself to the ground as the missile whanged by. He rose to his feet, marveling that he had not been trampled by his fellows behind him. Then he saw why. Half a dozen lay prostrate on the ground, four of them still, lifeless, the other two still moving feebly. But on either side the blue ranks were moving on, yelling like fiends now, the sunlight playing on bayonets as they dodged around trees, in and out of the shade. Here and there Johann saw a rebel, fleeing before the gleaming blades.

The men who had been serving the gun went down beneath a shower of blows. They looked strangely unsoldierlike, Johann thought as he passed the redoubt. One was an elderly, bald-headed man.

Just as he passed it, Johann heard another volley. But this one apparently was not from the enemy. No balls skittered through the trees this time. It must be Lord Percy's men penning the rebels by the attack from the rear!

As he ran, Johann stumbled and nearly fell over a musket lying on the ground. Then he saw another and still another. The rebels must be in rout! Even as he thought it, a fierce-throated roar went up from the woods all around. The cries of the wounded resounded as an awful undertone. The farther he went, the more fallen men he saw, some in the nondescript clothes of the rebels, others in the uniform of the Jägers or of his own regiment.

Now the Hessians gained the crest of the hill. Looking ahead, Johann could see, only a short distance away, the works of the rebel fort at Brooklyn! Between where he stood and a road farther on, he saw men fleeing madly toward the fort, most without weapons, some even without hats. He caught a flash of scarlet off to the right. Percy's troops, he thought, rapidly mopping up the fleeing enemy.

Now the yells and cries died down. Groups of Hessians were marching rearward, herding before them scattered bands of enemy soldiers. Again Johann noticed that most were not uniformed. Many were barely his own age. All seemed tired and frightened, unable to comprehend the commands given them, but seeming to know too well what the long bayonets of the grenadiers meant.

Here and there a surgeon's aide tended a wounded Hessian, or helped a limping one to the rear. Their proud blue uniforms were no longer bright, showed signs of dirt and of blood. The sun had long since passed the meridian and was moving slowly downward toward the horizon where Johann could see a wide bay and river and a fleet of ships, motionless. The bugle sounded again. The battle, the first battle, was over!

11

A FIRE

THE old woman in the faded green gown and tattered gray cap seemed frightened as she stood in the doorway of the yellow brick house.

It's plain she doesn't understand me, thought Johann. Again he repeated his question, gesturing to try and make up for his lack of English.

"Can you tell me where Herr Crainter lives hereabouts?"

The woman's head shook slowly from left to right.

Her beady eyes, squinting now and again against the September sun, looked him over from head to foot.

They're all alike, he thought. They're scared to death of us just because we don't speak their cursed tongue. Bet she thinks I want to rob her.

He tried again. More gestures. "Crainter, Crainter," he said. The old woman's face remained a pasty, frightened blank. Johann was about to go down the steps when he heard a hail from the tree-lined street.

"What's amiss, Corporal? Can I help you?"

Turning, Johann recognized Lieutenant Biehlte, one of General von Kohrn's aides.

"It's this blasted English," he replied. "I can't get it out. I'm looking for a man my father knew over here in New York. All I know is he lives somewhere near Water Street. That's it down that way, *nein*, Lieutenant?"

"That's it, Corporal," said the officer. "But this rabble won't tell us anything—whether they understand or not—now that we've taken their town. But let me try. What's the name of the man you're looking for?" Johann told him.

The officer and the woman talked for a few minutes, then the door closed, and the lieutenant joined Johann in the street.

"She says your Herr Crainter used to live in the next house but one." Johann's tanned face broke into smiles. But the Lieutenant went on, "She says she hasn't seen him since the day before we occupied New York. Says she thinks he went north with the rebel army when it retreated."

The boy hardly heard the officer's "Anything else I

can do for you?" He just mumbled his thanks and sat down on the bottom step to think.

So Herr Crainter was gone! It was too much to bear after all this time of dreaming and hoping. How or where would he ever find that watch of his father's and the map it contained?

Too tired and hungry to move, Johann sat for a long time, half noticing the townsfolk and the soldiers—red-coated British or blue-coated Hessians—going about their business. What should he do now? Of what use was it to him personally, he thought bitterly, that the King's army had three days ago taken the town almost without a shot? Now the rebel army had retreated again. And Herr Crainter was with them!

And it wasn't the first such maneuver. Two days after the battle on Long Island had ended, the rebel General Washington and his eight thousand men had given the royal army the slip. Taking advantage of a foggy August night, every man jack of them had been ferried over the East River to Manhattan Island and New York.

Johann had to smile to himself even as he remembered the incident. How General von Heister had raged! General Howe had been urged to attack the fort at Brooklyn while the rebels were recovering from the battle. But the British commander had refused, saying, "I won't risk men's lives needlessly."

It could be that he was too confident that the panicky foe, with about one thousand men taken, killed, or wounded in the battle—two of them Generals—would not hold out. But he had been wrong. Then, nearly two weeks had passed before the royal army followed to

Manhattan Island. Under the covering fire of the warships, Johann's battalion had led the way in a landing at Kip's Bay, midway the length of the island. The defenders had been routed again, thanks to the Hessians, and now the town was secure.

Meanwhile, the Americans, badly hit by desertions, were strongly entrenched on Harlem Heights, some miles to the north where the island rose to a considerable elevation. They had won a brisk skirmish momentarily the day after the landing. The British had been saved by a timely Hessian appearance on the scene.

Weary now, Johann started back to the house where he, Claus, Kampel, Baum, and Gorthalman, recovering from his wounds, were quartered. The two-story brick building was much more handsomely furnished than any Johann had yet seen. Even the inside walls were covered with paper in a design! The furniture was sturdier, richer, than any Johann remembered seeing in Cassel.

His comrades, who knew of his search for Herr Crainter, at once asked whether he'd had any luck. They all sympathized with him when he told his story.

"Never mind," said Claus. "Remember what Baum told us—that we'd make our fortunes here? From what I saw this morning, some of the lads are on their way to doing it already."

"What do you mean?" asked Johann. "The General has issued strict orders against looting."

"Orders!" snarled Gorthalman, trying to gesture with his bandaged arm. "Who obeys orders in a captive town? Do you think we'd get anything around here if we didn't take it? These people are getting richer every day we stay here. And the way Howe is acting, we'll be here forever.

"Why, if we didn't get the ships' provisions, a few moldy biscuits, some meat hardly fit to eat, a drop of rum now and then, we'd starve to death so far as these loyal citizens are concerned. Every time I've tried to buy something with my miserable few thalers, they ask three times as much!"

Claus and Kampel nodded in agreement.

"If we'd only get started toward Harlem while the weather remains good," put in the latter. "But no. It's wait for this. Wait for that. What do these British want? I heard only this afternoon the deserters from the rebel army are coming in dozens at a time. They can't have half the men we have in New York right now. Why don't we do something? Why?"

No one answered that question. In the silence that followed, a noise from outside forced itself on their attention.

"Hsst!" cautioned Gorthalman. "What's that?"

Claus ran to the open window and looked out.

"Hey," he called excitedly, "looks like the town is on fire! Come here, quick!"

Sure enough, as Johann looked out, a bright tongue of flame shot high in the air not a half-dozen streets away down by the North River. Now, borne on the strong evening breeze, they could hear the clamor of a crowd and the braying of fire trumpets.

"Come on, quick!" he yelled. "Maybe they need our help!"

Down the stairs they clattered, almost bowling Baum over as he entered from the street.

"Why the haste?" he rasped.

"Didn't you see it? The fire?" asked Claus.

"Oh, fire, is it? I heard a noise of some kind. I'm afraid after all the dry weather we've had, it's bound to spread fast. Sure, I'll go with you, lads. Can't tell what we might 'save.' " He laughed as he emphasized "save."

Twenty minutes later they found themselves on the edge of a murmuring, gaping, moving crowd. Even where he stood, Johann could feel the heat on his face. Fully half a street of houses was burning briskly, fanned by the wind.

A bucket brigade was working at one end of the nearest street. The sweating men handed along pails of water from a crude wagon surmounted by a big cask until the man closest to the fire could throw the water on the flames.

"Might as well spit on it," snorted Baum. "It's not goin' to stop here, neither." And he pointed upward to the showers of sparks sailing through the air, landing on every roof within sight.

Some soldiers and sailors, as well as townsfolk, were aiding the householders to move their clothes and furniture, piling them hastily in the middle of the street.

But just then a roar rose from the crowd. Johann looked around to see another group of soldiers, laughing and jostling one another, sprint toward the piled-up furnishings and begin to carry some of them off. Angry citizens began to close in on the roaring revelers,

94

some now pocketing small articles. One tottered along bearing a chair.

"Hey!" called Claus. "Those are some of our lads! They must be mad—or drunk—to try this! Hurry, lads! Follow me, else the dolts will have their skulls bashed in!"

Johann found himself butting his way through the crowd in the wake of Claus and Kampel. The nearer he got to the cursing, struggling soldiers and citizens, the slower was his progress. All around, the strange English tongue was raised in excited cries.

Then within feet of his objective, Johann heard another roar go up. Standing tiptoe, he saw a cordon of soldiers from the military guard arriving on the scene. They flailed away at both householders and soldiers alike, trying to break up the melee.

Then something thudded on Johann's head from behind. "Wait! Claus! Kamp—" and his voice trailed off. Darkness unrelieved by any leaping flame enveloped him, and he fell heavily to the slimy paving stones!

12

A FORCED JOURNEY

THERE'S a good lad. Open your mouth a bit more, boy. Here, here, now. Take it slowly."

Johann heard faintly, although he did not understand the words. But there was no mistaking the feel of a cup at his lips. Eagerly, for his mouth burned, he took a big gulp. Then he tried to open his eyes. But he shut them quickly again when a stabbing pain shot through his head.

All he could remember was watching the fire, the struggle through the mob, then a blow. Who had hit him? Who was this woman with the high-pitched English voice? Braving the throbbing pain, Johann opened his eyes.

His first dazed glance took in the woman standing over him, stub of a candle in hand.

"Where am I?" he asked. "Who are you?"

The woman was old, clad in a tattered gown much stained with grease and dirt. Her wrinkled face cracked in the semblance of a smile.

"Good," she said in English, "so you feel better, eh?"

Johann half gathered by her expression what she was saying, and in his own tongue asked her whether she spoke any German. Instantly, the smile disappeared. The woman looked cautiously about, put a dirty finger to her lips, then, pointing to a pitcher, turned slowly, opened a door, and left the shedlike room in darkness.

When she had gone, Johann sank back on the rough wooden floor. His aching head refused to answer the questions: How did I get here? Who is that woman? Why did she tell me to be still when I asked her if she spoke German?

For a long time he lay, hearing no sound. The pain in his head began to subside. Feeling thirsty again, he raised himself to grope for the pitcher she'd indicated. As he did his hand brushed the cup in the dark and sent it clattering along the floor.

Now he got to his knees. Where was that pitcher? He groped in all directions until at last he found its cool, rough sides. He had started to lift it to his lips when from the other side of the door he heard voices—men talking in his own language!

"Now listen well, old woman," the first voice began. Then, evidently talking to someone else, the man added, "Make sure she understands what I'm sayin', Kurt."

Another man's voice answered, "Yes, I'll translate for you."

"Now listen well, old woman," the first man began again. "I've paid you for hidin' me here in this rat trap. An' I want you to do what I tell you—no questions, understand?"

The second man spoke rapidly in English, the woman's voice said something, then the interpreter said, "She says she'll do what you ask."

"Well, then. Get me some clothes. I want somethin' to make me look like an American peddler. Hat, shirt, breeches, an' a coat of some sort. Nothin' fancy, mind you. An' get 'em back here in an hour. I've got to leave by then."

The voice sounded familiar. Who could he be? Why did he want to disguise himself? Something told Johann to wait to learn more before entering the other room. Now the interpreter was speaking to the woman. Johann heard her reply, heard a door slam, and then silence. She must have gone out.

All this, though, did not explain what he, Johann Leonhardt, was doing in this house, wherever it was. He must get out and report back to duty. But first, one more long, cooling drink. He raised the pitcher. But now the men were talking again.

"But," it was the interpreter's voice, "where can you go? Why risk everything now? You'll surely be caught."

98

"They'll never notice me," replied the other. "Everything's in an uproar since the fire. The people blame it on the King's soldiers. The soldiers blame it on the people. But they'll wish they'd left me alone—'specially if I can get through the lines to Harlem, believe me, Kurt. The Americans will pay well for the report I can give 'em about troops, supplies, plans, and stores."

"You're mad to try it," came the answer. "The army is bound to move on Harlem any day. And it will be only a matter of weeks before that British force from Canada cuts its way down to Lake Champlain and Albany. I tell you, the rebels' jig is about up."

The voices stopped. Johann took a long pull at the pitcher. The water tasted so good. Then the interpreter spoke again:

"Well, it's your neck, Ziggner. Not mine."

Ziggner here? Johann gagged on his drink. The pitcher fell from his trembling hands and dropped with a crash on the floor!

Steps sounded in the next room. The door was jerked open. And there stood Ziggner, one hand on the latch, the other gripping a pistol, peering into the room!

"Who's there?" he challenged. "Come out! Now! Or I shoot!"

At that moment Johann turned. His old enemy recognized him, and with a roar of rage sprang into the room. He seized Johann by the arm, dragging him through the door.

"The goose-livered clerk again!" he cried, spinning the lad around and into the second chamber. "Why must I always be plagued by you? Where, in heaven's

99

name, did you come from this time? Answer me! Did the old woman bring you here?"

But before Johann could answer, Ziggner was on him again. He pinned the boy's arms to his side with one powerful arm, and skillfully went through his pockets. Then, with another shove and a disgusted laugh, he turned on the other man, now cowering in a corner.

"Kurt! Kurt! Why didn't you keep an eye on her? D'ye know what she's done now? She's botched the whole thing! Now this pink-cheeked soldier boy knows my whole scheme!"

The gray-haired man in the tradesman's apron averted his eyes at Ziggner's raging tones.

"What, what do you mean?" he quavered.

"Mean!" shouted Ziggner, waving his pistol wildly. "I mean the old crone must a' discovered this brat lyin' drunk somewhere along Broadway after the fire. She must a' brought him here to pick his pockets! He ain't got a thaler on him!"

Johann felt in his pockets. It was true. His last bit of pay was gone. Even the trinkets he'd bought for his aunt were missing. He had been robbed, all right. Then the import of Ziggner's statement came to him. Johann grew warm all over.

"I never took a drink in my life, Ziggner, and you know it. Leastwise, I was never drunk. Someone hit me on the head while I was watching the fire. Then I knew nothing until I woke up and heard you talking to Kurt here."

Ziggner's face contorted again. He advanced, eyes glaring, until he stood inches from Johann. "Ha!" he snarled. "Then you did hear what I said? What my plans are? Well, my fine soldier boy, that settles it!"

"What if I did?" replied Johann. "I couldn't help that. You know I've done nothing. And if I don't get back to my post they'll put me on report as a deserter. You know that, Ziggner. Let bygones be bygones. Let me pass." And he started for the hallway door.

"Not so fast, Corporal," yelled Ziggner. "Thought I didn't notice you've been promoted, eh? Got that for tellin' on your friends again, eh? Well, you've turned me in twice. I'd be a fool to let you go! You've heard too much already! This time you've really cooked your goose!"

In the next moment, Ziggner seized Johann and hustled him back into the shed, banged and locked the door behind him. Johann was too stunned at this turn of events to fight back, but once in the shed it did not take long to determine that there was no other way out of it.

He returned to the door and began to bang on it lustily.

"Let me out! Let me out, Ziggner!" he called.

"Stop that caterwaulin', you milksop, or I'll shoot you through the door!" roared Ziggner. An ominous click followed this statement. Johann stopped his banging. Then he heard the outside door open and close and the old woman's voice.

"Fine. Fine. These'll do the trick," Johann heard Ziggner say. Then the shed door was opened, and Ziggner spoke once more:

"Come on out here, you whelp! I've got a new uniform for you!"

101

"Take off 'em clothes," he ordered the man named Kurt, who, protestingly, followed the command.

"Now you, Corporal, take off 'em fancy duds—an' put on Kurt's clothes," was the next order.

"You can't do this, Ziggner!" protested Johann.

"Oh, can't I?" retorted Ziggner, moving to Johann's side again. "Well," he said, and he brandished the pistol once more, "I got a friend here who says you're goin' to do it or there'll be a very dead Hessian corporal found here tomorrow mornin' when the watch comes around!"

There was something about the tone that told Johann Ziggner meant what he said, so without further parley, he removed his uniform and put on the old man's ragged garments.

"Now," ordered Ziggner, "outside an' keep right in front o' me. One false step, one cry to anyone, an' you'll wind up in the gutter again. But dead this time. March!"

For years after, Johann was to remember that strange journey. The streets were nearly deserted as they moved along. Here and there a soldier reeled his unsteady way back to his barracks or his quarters, but civilians were conspicuous by their absence. The townsfolk, thought Johann bitterly, know better than to be abroad at night in a captured town.

On they went, past taverns where the light glowed cheerily, where voices were raised in loud song, and laughter came plainly out into the mild September air. But only once did they pass a group of Hessians. As they approached, talking loudly, joking among themselves, Johann felt the barrel of Ziggner's pistol tighten against his spine.

"A word," hissed Ziggner in his ear, "an' you're finished!"

The soldiers passed by, one turning to give a friendly greeting.

Now the houses along the north road were becoming farther apart. Still no one halted them. The faint light of the moon, now that they were out of the town proper, cast deep shadows beneath the trees. The road gleamed like a dim white ribbon, stretching on through quiet fields where now and again the dimly seen shapes of farm animals loomed.

As they rounded a bend in the road, a campfire gleamed up ahead. Now, thought Johann, they'll discover the plan! For plainly, it was a British sentry point.

As they came nearer, Johann saw three sentries seated about the fire. At the sound of their feet, one of the three rose and faced in their direction, gun at the ready.

"Halt in the King's name! Who goes there?"

The pistol barrel pressed closer. Still Ziggner said nothing. Nearer and nearer they moved toward the campfire and the waiting sentry. Johann could see him now in the leaping flames. He was a young, blond youth, his uniform awry, his eyes not too steady.

"Halt!" he commanded again. "Halt, or I'll shoot!"

Now Ziggner waved something in his free hand, and never stopping until he had marched Johann under the sentry's nose, he handed over a piece of paper.

"What's the matter?" asked the sentry. "Can't you talk?"

"What's this?" he questioned, eyes wandering in a dazed way from the boy his own age standing before him to the grim, elder man standing close behind him. Without changing his stance the sentry called:

"Here, Matt, take a look at this paper, will you? They must be crazy in town to let these rebels wander around whenever and wherever they want to."

One of the other sentries put down the flagon he had been hopefully shaking, rose, and came over. He unfolded the paper, stared at it, then moved to the firelight to get a better look. As he did, Johann's first impulse was to cry out to the sentry, to tell him what Ziggner was doing. But in the next instant he realized he would be unable to make himself understood. And the pistol still pressed itself close against him.

"What's the paper say, Matt?" asked the first sentry.

"Says this fellow is a farmer from up Harlem way on his return from market in New York with his nephew. Says they was delayed after the signal. Funny thing, too, Sam. Says they're both dummies. Can't talk. Either o' 'em. 'Tis a pass signed by the adjutant."

The fire crackled in the still night. The third sentry suddenly lay down at full length and snored loudly.

"Look all right to you, Matt?" asked the first sentry.

"Aye. Might's well let'm go," replied the other. "What can a pair o' mutes tell the rebels, anyways? Let'm go, I say."

The soldier with the gun tried to look steadily at the faces in front of him. For a moment he hesitated, then said:

"All right. Pass!"

In another moment the campfire's light was lost in another turn in the road. Ziggner had passed his first barrier to the rebel lines!

For another hour Ziggner prodded Johann forward through the night. Then he turned in at a lane, at the end of which a farmhouse showed dimly in the waning moonlight, and ordered the boy to lie down behind a screen of bushes lining the lane.

"We'll not risk the rebel lines at night," he muttered. "They might shoot first an' ask questions second. So just lie still here till sunrise. An' don't think you're goin' to catch me fallin' asleep now. 'Cause I ain't."

For a long time Johann lay on the wet ground, listening to the sounds of the night breeze, the stirring of small animals in the dark. Then a cock at the farmhouse began to crow, and a faint streak of light appeared in the east. Ziggner sat not two feet from Johann, the pistol in his lap. The eyes never wavered in their watch.

When full daylight arrived, Ziggner poked Johann to his feet once more. The day was bright and warm as they moved steadily northward, passing now and then a farmer on his way to the town, but they saw no other sign of the people who Johann knew inhabited the farms along the rolling wayside. How rich a country it was, Johann thought. How lush the fields. How peaceful. It seemed hard to believe that behind and ahead were groups of men intent on killing each other!

Shortly after noon, as they came to a thicket, a ragged figure bounded out on the road before them. Aside from his tricornered hat, he did not look much different from any other American. But the long gun he carried, now brandished with purposeful intent, made it plain that he was an American outpost guard.

"Halt where yez are!" he called. And he turned and yelled into the thicket, "Come out, Mose. Here's two strange-lookin' critters."

Another tattered figure sprang from the leafy screen and advanced toward Ziggner and Johann.

Again, Ziggner uttered no sound, but, the pistol still jammed against Johann, waved another piece of paper.

The first sentry took it, looked at its bearer, then looked at the paper.

"Some writin' on it, Mose," he said in a slow drawl. "Can you read it?"

The man named Mose took the paper, screwed up his eyes, turned the paper over several times then spelled out slowly: "Pass bearer, a valiant friend of the cause, along to the first German-speakin' Pennsylvanian. He has information of importance for our army."

"Who signs it?" asked the first sentry.

"Can't make that out," he replied, "but it sez this feller's dumb an' the lad's his nephew. He's dumb, too. Maybe we'd better take 'em to Major Grant. He speaks the Dutchy lingo."

Minutes later, while Johann stood outside a farmhouse on the outskirts of the village of Harlem, Ziggner was taken inside. Through the open windows he heard Ziggner and an unseen man conversing in German, heard Ziggner assert that he must see a "principal officer" of the American army; that he had "valuable information" to give. The officer, a short, fat man in a blue and buff uniform came out, led Ziggner away, and told the man named Mose to take charge of Johann. The last Johann saw of Ziggner he was following at the major's heels along the road to Harlem.

13

A BATTLE ON A HILL

FIVE weeks later, as Johann took a rest from the
back-breaking job of shoveling earth for an American
rampart surrounding what the rebels called "Fort
Washington," he felt he knew what Ziggner had meant
when he said his "goose" would be "cooked."

It all seemed like a strange dream. A dream from
which he would waken to hear some rough, honest, German voices. Deserted by Ziggner at the outpost, unable
at first to make himself understood, Johann's lot had
not been an easy one.

For his clumsy efforts to explain in the few English words he half knew how Ziggner had forced him to accompany him, the rebels had only scorn and unbelief. And he had been led off to a guardhouse inside the fort. At first he did not know what might happen to him. He feared he might even be hanged as a spy by these bearded, rough, ill-clad men who called themselves soldiers. Johann had heard in New York that an American named Nathan Hale had recently been captured and hanged by the British for spying.

And for all his own silent amusement at the frantic rebel preparations for defending their fort, Johann had to admit to himself after seeing it, that they had chosen well for their citadel. It was so high that now, in the clear October air, Johann could look west across the sweep of the North River to the rocky cliffs of New Jersey on the other side. He could see Long Island off to the east, across the narrow Harlem River. Even farther off, he could see the blue waters of Long Island Sound. To the north, the country rose higher, but between it and the fortifications lay the swift course of Spuyten Duyvil, connecting the North River with the Harlem River.

The five-sided earthwork occupied a small space, actually. But outside its walls with their thirty-four cannon, lay surrounding chains of earthen redoubts, which, together with the sheer ascent from all but the Harlem side to the south, made it difficult to see how it could be assaulted easily. And three lines of earthworks crossed Break Neck Hill where the land sloped gradually upward from the Harlem plains.

As the first Hessian captive many of the Americans had seen, Johann had at first been none too gently treated. He had been poked at, kicked at, and even spat upon. But this ceased the day after he turned on one of his tormentors, a lad about his own age named Zack, and flailed him to the ground. They had been evenly matched at first, but Johann's longer training and his tremendous strength had finally overcome the slighter antagonist.

"Shake, Heshian," Zack had strangely murmured through puffed lips when the fight ended to the cheers of the other rebels. Johann did not understand the word, but could not misunderstand the gesture of the now friendly, outstretched right hand. A strange country, indeed, Johann thought afterward, when the fellow you knock down greets you with a handclasp.

In this and other ways, he soon found the Americans really bore him no personal grudge. They were, he discovered, inclined to be serious and uproariously happy by turns. He learned other things, too.

They were, for one thing, immensely proud of being Americans. And their dislike of authority didn't halt with a hatred of the British King and his soldiers. They even resented taking orders from their own officers at times. The latter had far less authority over the men than, say, a Hessian lieutenant. Their attempts at drilling were ludicrous, and, while they evidently knew how to shoot the poor muskets they possessed, they were far from Johann's own fellows in the way they executed military maneuvers on command. When they made mistakes they all laughed. Above all, they liked to talk of

110

their "freedom and equality" with anyone—even their own officers.

Then, unlike the Hessians, Johann found out, they weren't bound by hard and fast rules to serve in their army. When the enlistment period of some ran out, they just left, bidding good-by to their fellows, promising to go home to cut a few fields for them. Apparently many of them, like the boy Zack, were farmers who had interrupted their own work to fight.

"Hey, you, Heshian!" Johann heard the lanky, pipe-smoking man in charge of the work call. "Get busy with thet shovel. Ef'n you doan't, y'er friends will be able to walk in to shake hands with you." He was from the northern part of the country, Johann knew, but a kindly man for all his bark. The others standing around, or sitting on the ground smoking, roared at this joke. Johann began to dig again. But he had hardly taken a half-dozen shovelfuls, when a sudden stir ran through the fort.

The soldiers working with Johann immediately dropped their tools and ran off to join a group standing near the center of the citadel. Even Jeb, the overseer, went with them. Johann stopped working again and tried to catch what was being said. Apparently, someone was reading an order of some kind. There was a sudden shout from those gathered around. Some of the men started to jig about as though happy to hear the news—whatever it was.

It was not until the next day that Johann found out the reason. The British commander, after delaying any action for more than a month, had sent troops by boat up the East River and through Hell Gate, a treacherous stretch of that river, to land at a place called Throg's Neck, north and east of Manhattan Island. From this point the British were in a position to march west and cut off any rebel retreat from the island.

The orders Johann heard directed the twelve hundred Americans in the fortification to remain to defend it, while the rest of the army marched north to a village called White Plains to escape being trapped on the island. The men had been jubilant because they would not have to leave and would continue under the command of General Nathaniel Greene and Lieutenant Colonel John Magaw.

The next day, Johann heard more, this time while listening to Zack talking to another soldier. " 'Tis a good thing," he was saying, "Washington sent Glover's men over to meet 'em British an' Heshians near Pell's Neck, too. They'd a' jined up with 'em others an' cut all of us off, sure. I hear tell they gave 'em a run for their money. But consarn it, I doan't know what's a-goin' to happen to us."

The occupants of the fort did not have to wait long to find out what was "a-goin' to happen." For, a week later, the signal was given that a British warship was bound up the North River.

Johann saw it the moment he ran with the others to the westerly side. The October sun was glancing on her sails, her prow dashing up a white froth as she moved nearer.

Within minutes after she had been sighted, a runner brought news that Lord Percy's men were readying to attack the island from the north. Fort Independence on the heights across Spuyten Duyvil had been abandoned!

Johann's hopes soared. Maybe, he thought, they'll take the fort, and I'll be with Kampel, Claus, and Baum once again!

But the threat to the now isolated Fort Washington turned out to be more noise than action. Once the warship got within range of its cannon, of those on fortified Jeffrey's Hook below—as well as of those at Fort Lee across the North River—she abandoned her venture.

She had fired but a few salvos when the shore batteries got the range, and shot began to splash dangerously close to her. Just as the fire got the heaviest, Johann saw a group of the man-o'-war's sailors busy themselves about her anchor chain as though trying to draw it in, while a small boat was put off with a towline. The wind had changed, and the ship was unable to get herself out of range under her own power.

The batteries renewed their roar. The water around boat and ship spouted white now. It seemed that any minute a shot would strike home. Then the boat began to move slowly ahead, towing the vessel behind it out of harm's way. As the garrison set up a great "Huzza!" at the sight, Johann's hopes sank again.

But now came news from the North. The British had, after an inconclusive battle at White Plains, forced the Americans to withdraw again! The Americans were in retreat across the North River into New Jersey! Johann felt proud of his countrymen when he heard they had had a considerable part in this engagement.

"I doan't see how we're a-goin' to win this here war,"

said Zack a few days later, "ef'n we are always to be re-treatin'. They got more men 'n we have, anyways. Maybe, jes' like Gineral Washin'ton sez, they'll come after us in this fort." From his conversation, Johann gathered that not all the Americans were in agreement on leaving a garrison in Fort Washington.

But he appeared to have been right, when, a few days later, more men came pouring into the fort as rein-forcements. With their arrival, Johann felt sure it could withstand a siege, no matter how long. But as he looked around at the men piled helter-skelter, or shuttling be-tween the main stronghold and the outer works, he wondered to himself how they were even going to have elbow room to fight.

Then, on a November morning he was awakened by the roar of a cannon. Shivering against the chill, he hurried outside. The sun was just beginning to rise above the foggy haze that hung eastward over Long Island.

The New Jersey side of the North River was still half in the dark, the tall cliffs frowning down on the muddied waters. All at once that murk was lit by a flash, and in it Johann saw the outline of another British ship standing in close to shore.

Just outside his quarters, Colonel Magaw, com-mander of the fort, was conferring with his aides. He put a spyglass to his eye and directed it—not toward the river—but northward at Spuyten Duyvil and the place where the King's Bridge, the one good crossing between Manhattan and the mainland, lay.

Unnoticed in the noise, Johann moved closer and

listened. A ragged rebel soldier entered the gates on the dead run, burst in among the officers, and blurted out his message:

"Captin sent me to tell you Cornwallis an' a large body of men hev crossed the Harlem River in flatboats an' are advancin' to the batt'ry on Laurel Hill!"

The sun had surmounted the haze completely and now glared down in reddening splendor on the gorges to the east as Johann, trailing the officers, crossed to the other side and looked down at the Harlem.

Puffs of smoke rose from the Laurel Hill battery slightly lower than Fort Washington. Below that again Johann could see the red coats of the British soldiers, made redder yet by the sun, slowly struggling up the steep rise from the river. They were not firing, but advancing with fixed bayonets for a charge.

This, thought Johann, must be a real attack to take the fort at last! Now he realized it followed up the brief action of the day before when a British battery on nearby Fordham Heights had cannonaded Fort Washington for hours. This had been followed by the sending of a flag of truce through the lines and a demand for surrender.

"Your defense is hopeless," the resplendent British Guards' officer had told the Americans. "His Lordship is anxious to spare lives. The plans of your citadel are thoroughly known to us now—thanks to information brought us by one of your men three days ago. Your Washington and the rest of the army are scattered from here north to Peekskill and across the North River into New Jersey. It would be wiser if you gave up now."

The news that the plans had been disclosed by a traitor, Johann saw, came as a terrible shock to the rebel officers. For moments Colonel Magaw conferred with his aides, then returned to the triumphantly expectant Britisher. But his face quickly changed expression when Colonel Magaw said:

"You can tell your master he'll have to take the fort, bloodshed or not. We'll defend it to the last extremity."

Now to the rattle of musketry and boom of cannon from Laurel Hill was added a fresh, more distant outburst of firing—from the south. And almost at once the message came from the lines defending the approach up Break Neck Hill—Lord Percy was attacking from that side!

Johann permitted himself a quiet grin of anticipation. It widened to a smile when, a half hour later, another messenger reported two columns of Hessians under General von Knyphausen had crossed King's Bridge and were coming in from the north! My own regiment, exulted Johann! Now the fort was threatened on three sides, while on the fourth the warship kept up its steady fire. The air shook under the fire and counterfire, and the sun was nearly obscured by clouds of smoke pouring up from all sides.

Johann ran at once to the north side to see whether he could make out the Hessians. At first he could see nothing. As his eyes accustomed themselves to the drifting smoke, which first obscured, then revealed the autumn-colored tangle of bushes and trees masking the approach from Spuyten Duyvil, he saw, here and there, a rebel marksman cleverly concealed in a clump of bushes or perched in a tree's limb.

Next he saw the Hessians, their blue uniforms and the familiar brass headpieces glittering in the sun. They were toiling up the slope, slowly, oh, how slowly! The marksmen's guns were firing with deadly effect!

As he watched, one blue-clad figure after another spun and fell to the rough, rocky soil. Finally, the fire became so fierce the Hessians halted. Johann could see an officer striding up and down the lines, sword in hand, encouraging the faltering men.

Then to his ears came an unfamiliar wailing sound, reedy, high-pitched, followed by the rattle of a closer, newer volley in the direction of Harlem! A wounded rebel soldier staggered past him, mumbling to himself. Fear was written on his dirty, unshaven face. "The Highlanders, blast 'em!" he was saying. "Blast 'em an' their squeakin' bagpipes, too! They're cuttin' in behind the works at Break Neck Hill!"

Now the cannon on the north side began to fire again. Sweating for all the November chill, the gunners served the cannon well, sending showers of grape and shot down the steep hillside where the Hessians had resumed their upward march again. The crack and bang of the guns of the marksmen rang out from behind rocks and fallen trees. Again the blue-clad soldiers toppled in droves! But still their comrades came on up the hill!

They had reached a point where the terrain rose so steeply that only by gripping bushes, low limbs, or rock spurs were the Hessians able to make any upward progress at all! Johann saw one, in the act of seizing a bush, throw up his hands as he was hit, then go tumbling down on top of the men behind him. But another took his place, grabbed the same bush, and hoisted himself

up—to be followed by others! All along the rocky declivity the action was repeated.

From behind Johann now came a louder clamor. He turned to see hundreds of rebels, many without guns, come running through the fort's gate! These, guessed

Johann, must be the men driven out of the southern and eastern works by the British and Scots! Soon the enclosed space was a milling mass of fearful men whose officers seemed unable to discipline them. Now, on all sides, the firing grew louder, more insistent, closer! Johann threw himself down on the parapet and again turned his attention to the Hessians.

There, down the slope, apparently unworried about the deadly sharpshooters or the cannon on the earthworks still able to fire, stood a tall figure in the uniform of a Hessian colonel. Firmly, as though still on the parade ground, he was waving his sword toward the top, cheering his men on to continue the attack.

Whether it was his inspiration or a sudden slackening of fire, Johann couldn't tell, but suddenly the Hessian lines surged forward, firing by volleys. The white smoke clouded the nearer ranks, mingled with the black smoke from the fort's failing batteries. The volley fired, the men in blue fixed their bayonets and prepared for a final charge!

And in the next minute Johann saw the defenders of the outer works and some of the marksmen, leaping, jumping, over logs and rocks, running toward the fort! Right behind them came the Hessians, drummers sounding the beat, bugles blaring! Indeed, it was hard to tell where the enemy rear ranks ended and the forefront of the Hessian advance began!

The two bodies of men, inextricably mingled, moved forward in a wild melee. Now the first of the fleeing Americans clambered, breathing heavily, into the citadel. Others streamed in through the gate until its interior was one seething mass of men, some moving, others lying groaning on the cold ground, and still others gaping off to the North River, where the warship continued its fire.

The Hessian line halted to reform as it reached the level space just outside. Johann saw the Hessian officers grouped in front of the lines in conference. Then it broke up and a lone officer, accompanied by a drummer, stepped out—marching directly for the parapets! Something white fluttered in the still breeze. The sun had gone behind lowering clouds, and the white spot stood out distinctly.

As the two came closer, the rat-a-tat-tat of the drum could be heard above the sporadic firing from other directions. Then the regular throb of the drum was matched by the irregular cadence of shots from the fort. Not until Colonel Magaw ran to the parapet and ordered his men to cease fire on the flag of truce did it halt. Now Johann could see the flag was tied to a gun barrel carried like a flagstaff in front of the Hessian officer, a captain. He marched briskly along, unperturbed by flying bullets, a measured five paces behind the busy drummer.

Men by the hundreds stood on top of the works, as silent as the blue-uniformed lines outside. They watched as the captain and drummer were met by rebel soldiers outside the walls, blindfolded, and led around to enter the fort.

Through the hushed, watching Americans, the two were led to a spot not far from Johann, the bandages were removed, and the captain was presented to one of Colonel Magaw's subordinates.

"You've come to offer terms, Captain?" Johann heard the American officer ask.

"That's right, Major. I present the compliments of General von Knyphausen, who begs to inform you your position is hopeless. At this moment Lord Percy's men have taken the second line of your works below the fort to the south. General Cornwallis has complete possession of your battery and works on the east side—and, as you see—our men are without your very gate."

The eyes of the men moved toward the silent, waiting Hessian lines. There's no doubt of it, thought Johann, the lads made a brave show of it once they got to the top of the slope. These people will have more respect for a Hessian from now on.

"What are your terms?" asked the major.

"A worthy foe deserves the best," replied the Hessian officer with a slight bow. "The General asks that your men immediately march out and lay down their arms in front of our men. You are to tally all ammunition, provisions, and whatever belongs to your army. But you may retain all privately owned property."

The American officer returned the bow.

"Anything else, Captain?" he questioned.

"Yes. You are to hoist a white flag at once so that all our men and yours will know that fighting has ended."

How Johann longed to push his way through the crowd and present himself to the captain and the drummer! But something told him it would not be the right thing to do at this moment. The Americans must surrender! Already, many had been killed and wounded. There was now no source of water in the fort, for all of it had to be carried from a spring outside the walls. It would be sheer madness to refuse the terms!

The rebel major, his face grim, whispered to two of his aides. Then he said:

"Captain, we ask that we be given four hours to consider your terms."

The Hessian replied, "Not a minute longer than half an hour, Major." And with that he pulled a watch from his pocket, and stepped some distance away, the drummer shrinking at his heels as he marched under all the hostile eyes.

Paying no heed to the hubbub that broke out as soon as the American officer had left to confer with Colonel Magaw, the Hessian captain stood, watch in hand, looking about him. If he would only glance in my direction, thought Johann. It was just then that he heard an American near him say:

"You know what they do with you when you're taken prisoner, don't you?"

The half-dozen nearest him stepped even closer to hear his reply to the "What's?" that sounded about him.

"You're put aboard one of those old ships lying down the harbor, that's what. My brother was sent there when he was captured at Long Island along with General Sullivan. We haven't heard of him since."

There was a stir outside Colonel Magaw's quarters, and through the packed ranks came the colonel, followed by the major and the others who first talked to the Hessian captain.

"You Hessians make impossibilities possible," Johann and the quiet hundreds circling the knot of officers heard Colonel Magaw declare. "My fate is hard, but I believe I can do nothing other than accept your terms."

The Captain bowed, then said, "Colonel, it may be that the General himself will offer you better terms. If you care to accept my safe conduct to our lines, I'll try to get him to meet you."

Colonel Magaw looked quickly from one of his aides to the other, shrugged his shoulders, and directed the captain to lead the way. The drummer began his rat-a-tat-tat again, this time straightening up as though more sure of himself and correspondingly scornful of his foes. The procession marched through the gate, around the edge of the abatis, and from his vantage point Johann soon saw Colonel Magaw offer his sword to a Hessian general.

The colonel's subordinates came back within the fort. A bugle sounded, and, after some shouting of commands and considerable shuffling and grumbling, the rebel soldiers began to march out. The short November day was drawing to its close as the long rows of men wound out through the gate to the waiting Hessian lines.

The sun now burst through the gray clouds, shedding a single red beam across the North River, where the silent warship lay, across the level space where the Hessian regiment stood in rigid ranks. Somebody nudged Johann, and, turning, he saw the boy Zack, face streaked with dirt and powder, standing beside him. Once again,

Johann saw a familiar gesture. The grimy, cold-reddened hand was stretched out, the freckled thin face wreathed in a sad smile.

"You got us this time, Heshian," said Zack. "But maybe we'll do better the next." And he was gone, the last of the long line of Americans trudging through the gate. Now only Johann, the mustachioed grenadiers hunting for stray captives, and the wounded were left behind in what had so lately been such a crowded place.

Outside, as the first of the rebel prisoner file marched before the Hessian officers, their yellow, light blue, and white flags were being lowered to the ground. The passing captured soldiers were tossing their weapons on a growing stack.

Suddenly, the Hessians broke silence to cheer loudly. Wheeling, Johann saw a white banner, its folds reflecting the sunset's crimson glow, flapping at the top of a mast! The fight for Fort Washington was over!

14

SURPRISE AT THE TAVERN

IT was a joyful, boisterous meeting Johann had with
Baum, Kampel, Claus, and the others three days later at
a tavern in New York.

"Thought we'd lost you for fair," said Claus. "We
looked around after the fire and couldn't imagine what
had happened."

"Come on, lad," enjoined Baum, "eat up. You don't
look like all those weeks with the rebels put any fat on
your bones. How did they feed you, anyways?"

Johann told them the supplies to the fort had been

scanty. "They got most of their provisions from up-country and from Connecticut as long as they held possession of King's Bridge. After you took the bridge, the food got scarce. But tell me, how goes it with you? What have you been doing?"

Kampel, setting down his glass, looked at it for a minute, then answered, "Well enough. Considerin' we nearly had our comeuppance at Pell's Point, whilst you were restin' in the rebel fort. The rebels fairly had us trapped along a hollow way when old Howe figgered we could just get behind 'em and bottle 'em up on Manhattan Island." He sighed. " 'Twas touch an' go for a long time. Many of the lads who sailed up the East River six weeks ago will never go back to Hesse-Cassel."

The questions then turned to Ziggner. Johann told them that after the arrival at Fort Washington he'd never seen the man again. It was Claus who supplied what little information was to be had about him. "He was put in irons under special guard the day we landed," Claus said. "For some reason, they never did get around to passing sentence on him.

"The next thing I heard," Claus continued, "he'd complained of some sickness and asked to be transferred to the sick quarters. There, they tell me, he bribed someone and just walked out."

"He'll turn up again, somewhere, mark my word," growled Kampel. "An' if he does, an' I see him first. . . ." And his big fist crashed down on the table, bouncing the dishes about.

After supper the friends told Johann what had happened since his capture. A British force, accompanied

126

by a Hessian army had chased the rebels north to White Plains, where the Hessians had again saved the day by shoving determined rebel regiments off Chatterton's Hill. More Hessians had been killed than Americans, and after the battle, the rebel forces withdrew, many of them moving across the North River into New Jersey.

"How much longer they can keep it up, I can't tell you," commented Baum. "Daily their enlistment terms run out. An' then they just up an' leave camp. Washington can't have more than six thousand men by now."

"But there's still a lot up in Westchester, north of here," reminded Claus, "and around that fort at West Point up the river."

A goodly part of the Hessian forces had been taken along with Britishers under Lord Cornwallis to chase the dwindling American army south into New Jersey, Baum told Johann.

"But we're still here in New York," he added. "Why don't we go down to that house where Ziggner caught Johann an' get that old woman to give up the money she took from him?"

They all roared with laughter at the suggestion. Baum first protested he was serious, then joined in the laugh. "Well," he said, "maybe you're right. There's enough to be had in this town without takin' it from an old woman."

After he went to bed that night, Johann's thoughts turned to Herr Crainter, and he wondered what had happened to him and the watch. He remembered how he had been told his father's friend had gone to Harlem.

At that time, though, the British had occupied the island only as far as the eighth milestone. Now they possessed the entire island, including the village. Why not, thought Johann, go to Harlem and see for himself if he could find Herr Crainter?

The next morning he presented himself to the officer on duty, explained that he wanted to be relieved of duty for the day, and told him why.

The elderly officer looked Johann up and down. He saw a sparely built youth nearing eighteen years, standing straight and tall before him, hands by his side, uniform neat, boots shining. The blue eyes were shining, too.

"Well," he garumphed, "I suppose I can hardly deny you a day's leave since you are of the town garrison. After all, you have been in the rebel camp, a prisoner. But be back here for roll call tomorrow morning, or it's the guardhouse for you."

Johann had started out the door when he heard the officer say in lowered tones, "But mind you, watch out for yourself. The British are too busy in town with their own affairs. Affairs like stealing books and selling them for a drink. Most of our men are scrounging around for something to eat. There aren't too many soldiers up in Harlem. You'd better watch out for the outlaws."

Johann returned to his quarters, grabbed a portion of bread and some cheese, stuffed them in his pockets, and hunted up Claus to tell him where he was going.

"Well," said Claus, "I guess it's safe enough. With Fort Lee over in New Jersey abandoned, and Washington's men well across the Hackensack and Passaic Rivers, there's little chance you'll have any trouble. They say General Charles Lee's army is still on this side of the North River, but he's too far away to bother about. Just remember, look out for the outlaws."

"Lieutenant Wobbe told me about them, too. What or who are they?" asked Johann.

"They are irregulars. Men of no party, no army, no principle. After one army has overrun a piece of land, they pretend to be friendly with that army and persecute any and all they say are its foes. If another army moves in and drives out the first, then they pretend to be friendly with the second. In this way they rob and murder defenseless people under the pretext of legal war. And the soldiers in both armies, British and American, get blamed for what these outlaws do."

The second journey to Harlem was much more pleasant than the one with Ziggner. Although it was nearing December and the weather had turned quite cold, the brisk walk through the rolling countryside dotted with mansions and estates of the town's wealthy, was enjoyable now.

But Johann's search proved more difficult than he had imagined. While he now knew enough English to make himself understood, the sound of his voice, and more, the sight of his uniform, was enough to shut doors in his face for all its youthful and open expression.

The sight of a woman at one house shrinking inside the door and clutching her little girl when she saw the uniform gave Johann an uncomfortable, angry feeling. What he thought, is wrong with these people? Do they think I'm going to rob them? Steal their possessions? Or don't they know His Majesty's forces, aided by his loyal Hessians, now hold the land from New York almost to the rebel capital in Philadelphia?

Despairing of a door-to-door hunt, Johann approached a man working in a nearby field. Of him he asked the questions he'd been asking for an hour: "Did you ever hear of a man named Crainter in Harlem? Do you know where I can find him?" The man barely halted his labor, looked Johann over carefully, then nodded his head. Johann's heart skipped rapidly.

"Where is he now?" he asked.

"If he's anywhere around here yet, you'll find out at the tavern down there on the road leading to the Heights." And the farmer resumed his work.

The inn was not very old. A freshly painted sign hung outside. On it a tree was drawn crudely, and underneath the tree, the word "Liberty."

Johann thought nothing of it. He had seen such symbols from one end of the town to the other. So he pushed open the door and entered. The tavern's interior was bright and clean. A fire burned briskly on the ample hearth. Several men sat at the tables scattered around the sanded floor of the common room.

The conversation he heard as he opened the door died the minute he appeared. A serving man looked up and slowly put down the drinking mug in his hand. Johann felt his face flush as he clumped forward. He was conscious of how loud his boots sounded.

"Stop where you are," ordered the servingman. "We serve none of the King's men in this tavern, 'specially none o' his hirelings an' slaves, the Hessians."

A murmur of approval rose from those at the tables. They were all staring at Johann. He fumbled for the few English words he knew. What did "hirelings" and "slaves" mean, he wondered. Weren't the Hessians as good, aye, better soldiers so far at winning battles, as the Redcoats? Johann forced down his anger and asked his question. A man had directed him to the tavern to find out about Herr Crainter, he explained.

A big man in a black cloak, seated at one of the tables began, "Why yes, I know—" when a sudden nudge from his neighbor silenced him.

All this while, the servingman continued to wipe his mugs. When the big man's sentence had been cut off short, he spoke again, "I said, we don't serve no Hessians in this tavern. Get out."

Furious, Johann wheeled and walked up to the cloaked man. The man pulled the garment closer about him and turned in his seat so his back was to Johann.

"You, sir," began Johann. "You seem to know something. It is important that I find this Herr Crainter. Can you tell me aught of him?"

Still the cloaked man remained silent. Johann heard a sudden whispering behind him and whirled to see another of the customers, an old man in too tight small-clothes, tiptoe away from the servingman's side. He disappeared through a back door while Johann watched, baffled.

To Johann's surprise, the servingman now started to smile. He motioned to the boy to approach him, and at the same time held out a brimming mug of ale to him. "Maybe I made a mistake, Hessian," he said. "You've

131

had a long walk. No doubt ye're dry. Here, have a swallow on the house."

Johann looked from him back to the cloaked man, then around at the others. Why, he wondered, this sudden change? But as he saw the foaming mug, he decided to accept, particularly as at that moment hunger struck him. He remembered his bread and cheese, took them out, and with the mug walked back to a table and sat down.

Only when he did so, did he realize how tired, cold, and hungry he was. The heat of the fire now made itself felt. It was good to rest, eat, and be warm again. But now, one by one, he saw his silent tavern mates rise, make an elaborate show of paying their score, and go out through the front door. Only one spoke. He of the black cloak threw a short "Good day to you, Aaron," as he left.

The afternoon's light was waning. Much of the pleasant common room was in shadow, a shadow fitfully illuminated by the hearth's fire. Aaron continued to busy himself about the tap, never lifting his eyes from his work.

Johann finished his food and the ale. He rose, hating to leave the comfort of the tavern for the long walk back. He turned for the door, but before he reached it, with a quick leap and lithe step, Aaron interposed himself between Johann and the door. He raised a finger to his lips for silence. Then, still moving with catlike tread to the door, he opened it, looked out, and shut it again.

He approached Johann again, the black eyes in the

132

pale face blinking rapidly, the fingers twining and untwining themselves in the dirty apron.

"Do you know," he began in a curious, husky voice, "this Crainter you inquire about?" And then: "Why do you seek him?"

"But I thought," began Johann, overcome at the sudden question, "you said you weren't interested in having anything to do with Hessians. You wanted to throw me out not a quarter hour ago."

The eyes blinked faster. Aaron looked over his shoulder toward the rear door, then, pushing Johann down in the nearest chair, said:

"Listen, Hessian. I'm playin' a devil's game here. I'm sorry for what I said awhile ago—but I had to. George III, God bless him, has no more loyal subject than Aaron Cole. Why, right now, my brother, George, is fightin' wi' Cornwallis over in New Jersey. Now tell me, is this Crainter, or whatever his real name is, a tanner by trade? A little bit o' a man missin' the one hand, the left?"

Stunned by suddenly coming on someone who had actually seen his father's missing friend, Johann was barely able to reply. "I never saw him myself. He was my father's friend here in New York. Have you seen him? Do you know him? Where is he?" The questions fairly rained on one another.

Another quick look at the doors, and Aaron bent closer. "Listen," he said, "this is no place for you. Take my advice an' get back to New York!"

"But why? Why do you say that?" asked Johann.

"Because, within the hour, if my rebel friends are

133

right, the leader of the outlaws hereabouts will be here. That old man you saw leave here is friendly wi' 'em. An' they, 'specially him, might not take kindly to findin' you here."

"But what . . . what has that to do with Herr Crainter?" asked Johann.

Now the servingman's breath was on Johann's cheek. "About three weeks ago, it was, Crainter was here." He halted at Johann's expression of surprise and went on. "Y'see, unbeknownst to all but meself, Crainter was a British secret agent. He'd been behind the American lines pickin' up information an' was on his way back when he stopped in.

"Well, whilst he was here, the outlaw leader came in, too. An' before I got wind o' what was up, one o' the Americans in the place denounced Crainter as a King's man. One word led to another, an' before I knowed it, the outlaw chief was threatenin' to turn Crainter over to the Americans as a spy. But this outlaw, a sly one he is, lets on that for a price he'll forget what was said. An' the next thing I knowed, this Crainter puts a big watch on the table—"

"A watch?" cried Johann.

"Shh, man. On yer life! Be still!" grated Aaron. "Yes, a watch. Ye mind, I can't pertend I'm any friend o' Crainter's, an' so whilst I'm watchin', this here Crainter hands over the watch to the outlaw leader."

"Go on," muttered Johann, fearing what he might hear next.

"Nothin' more right then. But about a half hour after Crainter leaves, someone comes in yellin' that he'd

134

been found dead—lyin' in a ditch alongside Break Neck Hill. Money gone, most o' his clothes stole."

Johann sank back in the chair. Herr Crainter dead! The watch gone! What could he do now? How could he ever prove his title to the property his father's friend had deeded? Then he told Aaron his story—how the clues to whatever estate his father had left, as well as the map to the property, were all left to Herr Crainter; how he had hoped to recover both by meeting the tanner.

"But now he's dead! Now this outlaw chief has the watch!" moaned Johann. "What can I do? How can I ever get the watch back from him?"

Aaron stepped quickly to the window, looked out, then replied, "I'm right sorry to hear it, lad. But a whole skin's better than any property or estate in these times, if you were to ask me. If I was you, I'd get out o' here an' forget the whole thing."

But hardly had he said it when a clatter of hoofs sounded outside. Aaron dashed to the back door, then cried: "It's them! The outlaws! Come the back way, they did." The words fairly jerked out of his twisting mouth. "Here! Quick! Through that door an' up the stairs! Lay low an' don't breathe till you hear 'em go! Hurry, now!"

From a tiny-paned window, Johann looked out to see three men dismounting in the rear of the tavern. They were just barely visible in the gathering darkness. Then, as the foremost reached the door and opened it, Johann nearly cried out in surprise. For the second man, now plainly seen in the light was—Ziggner!

Was Ziggner the outlaw leader Aaron had mentioned? If he was, then Ziggner—Johann's sworn enemy —had his father's watch. Scarcely daring to breathe, Johann crouched, listening to the noises in the room below.

"Well, Aaron," he heard Ziggner say. "Trade not so good since His Majesty—curse him—and his men took Fort Washington, eh?"

Johann couldn't catch the reply made by Aaron.

"Give us a drink, Aaron," a second voice said.

There was a brief silence below, then Ziggner's voice rose again: "He's kinda slow, ain't he, boys? Shall we hurry Aaron a bit, eh?" Johann heard Aaron give a cry of pain, loud laughs from the three, then the clink of a sword. Another silence, then: "Maybe he's savin' his drinks for his friends, eh, boys?" It was Ziggner's voice again.

Then a bottle crashed. A sound of struggling rose from the common room, heavy breathing, and another anguished cry from Aaron. "All right! All right! Don't do it any more! I'll tell you! Don't! He's, he's upstairs!"

Johann heard the hall door slam open, heard heavy footsteps ascending the staircase. It took but a moment to kick out the glass of the window, lift one leg over the sill, then the other, hang for a moment, and drop to the ground!

Even as his hands slipped over the rough sill, the steps sounded outside the room door. Scrambling to his feet, breathless but unhurt, he paused for a second. If, his mind raced, I try to escape on foot, they'll take me surely. There was only one chance.

In another moment he was at the side of the tethered

horses. He'd never ridden one before, but somehow got himself on the back of the first, loosened and kicked the other beasts into flight, then booted his own animal!

A flash, next an instant report, came from the window. The ball whizzed past his head. Scared by the noise, the horse redoubled its speed without any urging. In another minute he had rounded the inn and was headed back toward Bloomingdale and New York, safely hidden by the night!

15

GUARDING AN OUTPOST

BEHIND him, in the cheery comfort of the house and shop that had once belonged to a rebel tradesman, Johann could hear the laughter and shouts of his luckier fellows.

How he wished he had his father's watch! Then, he thought, at least I'd know how much longer I have to stand out here in this cursed winter weather!

A month had passed since the night he fled on Ziggner's horse, but he had heard nothing more about the outlaw. Johann had thought of asking the captain to get him a detail of men and of returning to Harlem to search for Ziggner and his band. But the plan had been abandoned when the entire Hessian contingent had been ordered across the North River into New Jersey to aid General Cornwallis' army in his pursuit of the fleeing American army.

"Leave it to Ziggner!" Baum had exploded when he heard Johann's story about his adventure at the Liberty Inn in Harlem. "First, he escapes bein' shot like a traitor; then he gets out o' havin' to fight with us at Fort Wash—excuse me, Fort Knyphausen, as 'tis now called; then, somehow, bless me if I can figure out how, he escapes from the Americans before we get into the fort, an' joins up with this band of renegades!"

"Yes, an' probably gettin' rich on the pickin's while we have to stick it out in this town an' scrounge for enough to eat," growled Kampel, gnawing away at an apple he'd bought.

But to Johann all that seemed long ago now, as for the tenth time he brushed the heavily falling snow from his shoulders and hunched himself deeper into his coat. Almost he wished he was Ziggner's horse, now probably bedded down comfortably in a nice, warm, dry stall, maybe even sleeping.

Strangely enough, the horse is really the reason for my being here, Johann thought. I might have been in Princeton or New Brunswick, instead of guarding a freezing outpost on the outskirts of this half-deserted village of Trenton.

For the day after he had returned to New York from Harlem, the horse, a big chestnut, had taken the eye of

Colonel Johann Rall. The colonel had summoned him to his quarters and offered him a price for the animal—and also offered him a transfer to his regiment.

This Colonel Rall was a quick-tempered old soldier, red of face and given to strange Turkish oaths when excited. He'd picked them up while serving with the Turks against the Russians. And when the Hessians left New York shortly after the first of December, Johann marched in Colonel Rall's regiment—and with him went Kampel, Claus, and Baum, transferred, too, at Johann's request.

Even as a boy in his native land, Johann could never remember such cold and snow! It had been coming down steadily for three hours, the first heavy fall of the winter. How cold his toes felt in the hard boots, now covered over the instep with the powdery stuff!

But orders were orders. Even though the rebel army —or what was left of it—had retreated across the Delaware River to the south weeks ago, there was no telling when a scouting party, or even a heavy, desperate thrust might materialize. At least that's what he'd heard Colonel von Donop tell Colonel Rall the day before.

At the thought of that peppery debate between the two veteran officers, Johann blinked his eyes and tried again to look west down the Pennington road. But the driving snow made visibility practically impossible. Anyway, who but a poor Hessian picket would be out on a night like this?

At that moment, a flood of light fell across the snow in front of him, the laughs and conversation of his fellow picket members became momentarily louder, and in another minute Kampel was at his side.

"Your relief reportin', Captain Snowman," grumbled Kampel. "Don't forget to tell Claus he's my relief, an' not to wait half the night to come out here."

Stiff, aching in every joint, and hardly able to lift his musket butt out of the gathering snow, Johann mumbled:

"It's all yours, complete with snow and icicles. Keep an eye out for the rebels. And don't go to sleep."

"Ha!" snorted Kampel, arranging his coat, hat, and blanket to protect him from the snow. "Lot of sleepin' a man will do out here this night."

Twenty minutes inside the cooper's snug house before the roaring fire and Johann felt himself again. He sat quietly before the hearth enjoying the warmth while round the room the rest of the pickets sat playing cards, fitfully snoring, or just talking.

"Look at this," one of his new regiment fellows was telling another; "this is what I picked up at Hackensack."

"Ho! Ho! Hackensack!" roared the other. "Do I remember that place! We sure had the rebels on the run that day! If Cornwallis had moved faster, we'd a' bagged them all when they crossed the river, an' wouldn't be sittin' here. We might be enjoyin' Christmas in New York."

"Did you ever see such stuff?" insisted the other, unrolling a tattered blanket. "I got it after the town 'caught' on fire. Look! Two silver watches, three sets of silver buckles, a pair of women's cotton stockings, two fine tablecloths, and a silver teaspoon. Yes, and five Spanish dollars and other money."

The other spat disgustedly into the fire. "That's nothin'," he said. "You should see what I had to throw away when we took off again after the Americans! When I think of it! Eleven pieces of fine linen an' over two dozen silk handkerchiefs, six silver plates, an' a drinkin' mug. Silver it was, too."

Nearby Baum was talking to another of their new mates.

"What I can't understand," he was saying, "is why we couldn't find even a few boats somewheres along the Delaware! The rebels couldn't have gone off with every boat in the countryside. We looked for more than three days."

"How well I remember," answered the other. "An' the captain made us march along the river twice just to make sure. Brr. It was that cold, with big chunks of ice floatin' down the river."

"Yes, an' if we'd a' found some boats we'd a' been over it right behind Washington when he crossed three weeks ago. Now the cursed river will neither freeze nor unfreeze, an' we can't get across. Cornwallis, they tell me, thinks the rebels will stay there for the winter. At that, I guess it's all they can do. I heard Rall tell the captain the Americans couldn't have more than five thousand men—an' that about half of 'em will leave—as they alway do when their enlistment is up—just about New Year's."

"Oh, well," yawned the other, "if we can't get across it, neither can they. At least not more than a small party or two. An' if they try anythin', our thousand here, together with von Donop's men at Bordentown an' the English at Princeton an' New Brunswick should be able to beat 'em off."

"Just the same," rejoined Baum, "I wish I was back in New York with Howe and von Heister. A great commander of Hessian troops he is, sittin' comfortably in a fine town while we freeze out here."

Thus it went, day after day, night after night. Standing guard, parading, freezing, warming up, telling and retelling stories of the long chase after the rebel army from the Hudson to the Delaware. And still no signs of a move from the foe across the ice-dotted river.

One day not long before Christmas, Johann was in the building used as a stable for officers' mounts, caring for the horse he'd sold Colonel Rall, when he heard angry voices outside. The blustery voice of the little colonel came plainly to him.

"Earthworks, Major!" he exclaimed. "What's the use of putting them up at this time of the year? Von Donop's man was here a week ago and told me the same thing. Earthworks! Earthworks! You'd think I didn't know my business! I've taken precautions, you know. We've got men down at the bridge over the Assanpink Creek and a picket out near the Pennington road. The von Lossberg regiment and my own are quartered north of the creek, the von Knyphausen regiment south of it. I just wish they'd try something. I'd like to see that old fox, Washington, come over here. I tell you, he'd no sooner cross than he'd be captured."

Colonel Rall and the other officer walked on, and

Johann went to the door to watch them go up King Street, one of the two parallel, principal streets in the small town. Even as he watched, he heard the sound of music on the frosty air, and around the church came the nine-piece regimental band, tootling bravely on fifes and trumpets, beating lustily at their drums.

Johann couldn't help smiling when he heard and saw the band, followed as it was by the children of the few families who had chosen to remain behind after the rebels crossed the Delaware. It was one of the colonel's favorite occupations to march the band around and around at parade time, at any time! How the colonel loved the familiar martial airs of the old country! And how the children, unconscious of what these strange men meant, danced along in time to the music.

A British cavalryman clattered up just then to the stable. He tossed the reins over his mount's steaming neck and jumped to the ground right in front of Johann.

"Where'll I find Colonel Rall, Corporal?" he asked.

Johann told him, and the mounted man, running stiffly in his heavy boots, disappeared up the street. In ten minutes he was back, muttering to himself. Then he addressed Johann again.

"Where'll I get something to eat? Can't start back to Princeton with my horse in this shape. Curse these Hessians for blockheads."

Johann seized the reins and led the horse into the building, the British soldier following him, still mumbling.

144

"What's the matter, Britisher?" Johann asked. "Can't stand the sight of your betters?"

"Betters, my foot!" snapped the other. "I just brought a message from our General Leslie telling you Hessians to be on the lookout for the rebels instead of just sitting around. And what do you think the great Colonel Rall told me? Why, he said, 'Washington won't come within a mile of any Hessians! He knows better after White Plains and Fort Washington.' Just like that."

"Do you think the rebels will cross the river?" asked Johann, beginning to rub down the horse. "What can Washington do with the few men he's got?"

"Do?" replied the Britisher. "He'll do plenty if he gets the chance, particularly now that he has at last gotten Lee's men across with him."

Johann had heard that the American General Lee had remained across the North River and aloof from Washington for weeks. "How do you know that?" he asked.

"Because just last week, whilst you Hessians were playing at soldier here, some of our men captured Lee within three miles of the rebel lines. We got him all right—but his army, the one he brought down from York State—got across to join Washington, something like three thousand men, they tell me."

Johann repeated this bit of news to Baum later. But the veteran only scoffed at the news. He was more inclined to blame the British for letting the army get through.

"An' all they took was a general, was it?" he asked.

"An' a renegade one at that." He explained that General Lee had once held a commission in the British King's army.

"Mighty little good 'twill do 'em," he said. "They'll just freeze an' starve over t'other side o' the river with the rest. They can't do us no harm."

"But," rejoined Johann, who had thought of it often since Colonel von Donop's man visited Trenton, "we haven't got so much as an earthwork to defend the town. Our cannon are all placed at one spot—right by Colonel Rall's house. And you know that aside from that letter-carrying expedition, we haven't sent out a scouting party in days." He paused, then added, "How do we know what they're doing over there? Maybe, if we couldn't find any boats, it means they have them. They could cross and not find a thing between the river and Trenton to stop them."

But Baum snorted at this idea. "The Colonel knows his business," was his only reply. The "letter-carrying" Johann mentioned had come about this way: A small band of Americans had, a few days before, killed one or two of the regiment on their way to Princeton with a letter. But when Colonel Rall had sent out a detachment, complete with cannon, to carry the same letter, no further signs of the foe had been seen.

Christmas Eve came, and preparations for the celebration of the holiday brought no new indications of what the enemy might be up to.

Johann, in common with the rest of the regiment, enjoyed the holiday rations and the brave attempts to hold a Yuletide the next day. But like everyone else, he

146

couldn't help thinking how much better it would be to be back in his native land instead of watching for an enemy that never appeared in strength in a strange countryside, thickly wrapped in ice and snow.

Thoughts of home and of Herr Gottfriend led naturally to wondering about the watch and what had happened to it. Where, thought Johann, was Ziggner now? Did he still have the watch? As he looked around him at his fellows trying to make the most of their poor holiday, Johann found himself wondering, too, what the rebels were doing on this holy feast day? Would they be able to make merry? Maybe, he thought, they are right now drinking to the season, certain that their cause is right. Drinking to their Congress, as they called their leaders, to their General Washington. Both sides toasting early victory. But only one could be right. Why, thought Johann, should that be?

Bracing himself against the weather, Johann later that day left the merriment at the house on Queen Street, crossed to King, and went to the cooper's house to report for picket duty. The sun had long set, but there were no stars out. A dank chill hung in the biting air. It looked like more snow. As he turned in for the night he could hear his companions still singing the old country holiday hymns. Merry Christmas, he thought. What a joke!

A hand shook Johann's shoulder hours later. Shivering and yawning, he crawled from beneath his blanket, warmed himself briefly at the still-glowing fire, and went outside. The snow was coming down again, heavily, this time mixed with sleet. It rattled on his helmet

147

and pelted at his face as he stepped forward, slipping and sliding, to relieve the guard.

The man on duty, numb and sheathed with snow and ice, barely acknowledged the relief. As he creaked away toward warmth, shelter, and sleep, he mumbled something that Johann didn't hear in the shrilling of the wind. Johann took up his post. Trying to keep his eyes fully open to watch up the Pennington road was too much of an effort. So he closed them until they were mere slits. Then the eyelids threatened to close up entirely under the relentless sleet.

Shivering, stamping his feet, and crunching back and forth to keep warm, somehow he managed to pass the next few hours. At last, when he felt that there no longer was a warm bone in his body, his relief came. He just managed to make the house, almost fell across the threshold, and tumbled into his bed. From somewhere in the town, over the patter of the sleet he thought he heard voices singing. Must be still celebrating over at headquarters, he thought sleepily. Must be nice to be an officer and not have to stand watch on nights like this. Then warm slumber overcame him.

16

DEATH IN THE SNOW

OW long he slept that night Johann never remembered afterward. A sudden swift blow in his back had awakened him to realize that it was faintly daylight and that a confused shouting was coming from somewhere outside.

"Up! Up, lad!" It was Baum, standing over him, buckling his belt and tightening his uniform at the ⸻ ⸻ ket just reported sightin' some men! It ⸻ rebels at last! Comin' down the Pennington ⸻ Quick, now! Hurry!"

Johann sprang to his feet, gathered his gear, and had just started to pull on one of his boots when a roar came plainly to him:

"Out! Out! To arms! The rebels are on us!"

The small room was chaotic now. Men ran excitedly about, bumping into each other in their haste. Helmets and guns clattered and clashed. Then, still tugging at uniform fastenings, they began to run for the door. As Johann leaped out behind Claus and Kampel, with Baum following, he saw the snow was still coming down, now heavily mixed with sleet. The trees up toward the Pennington road were coated with ice and shone dully in the morning's half-light.

The captain and the picket were about fifty yards from the house. The picket, sheathed in snow, was pointing toward the road, the one that Johann knew led back south and west to the Delaware River crossing at McKonkey's Ferry. Actually, it divided outside Trenton, and the other branch, known as the River Road, entered Trenton at its south end.

Johann glanced toward it as he ran to form in line. Yes, there they were. A dark line of men filing out of the woods from the northwest. They were moving slowly toward where he and his fellow Hessians stood shivering in the driving storm.

This was more than a reconnoitering party! More and more of them emerged from the forest. Several were mounted; some were drawing what appeared to be cannon. This, thought Johann, must be it! This is what we've been waiting for!

"Claus," ordered the captain, "run back to Colonel

Rall's quarters and tell him the enemy is advancing in force. It may be a major attack, tell him. And here, Claus," the captain fumbled beneath the skirt of his uniform, "take this message with you. A native delivered it to the picket not twenty minutes ago. It's written in English, but I can't read it. It may be important. Have somebody translate it. Off with you now, and tell him we'll hold as long as we can."

Claus started on the run through the snow, slipping and sliding over the ice-encrusted surface. His helmet fell off as he ran, but he plunged on.

"Make your pieces ready," ordered the captain. "And don't fire until I give you the word!"

With stiffening fingers, Johann arranged the priming, tested the powder. Still dry. That was one blessing. The advancing foe was not more than a thousand yards away. Now eight hundred yards separated the two ranks. Now five hundred yards. Above the patter of the sleet he could hear the crunch of massed feet in the snow, the grunts of the men pulling the cannon in traces.

He heard a command, an English spoken command, ring out, and, feeling as though he were gazing at a picture and not really in it, he watched while the rebel ranks formed up. The clatter of muskets sounded. Muzzles were raised in ragged unison. Then another command.

Through slitted eyes Johann saw a burst of smoke and heard a sharp, irregularly spaced series of reports. The zing of musket balls sounded over his head, and a

151

shower of ice-coated twigs clattered to the frozen snow. The rebel volley had gone high!

Now the rebels were reloading, still holding the same position. No nearer. Yet the captain stood motionless, watching. Again a command, again a burst of sound swiftly carried away by the wind. But once more the aim was too high. How long would the captain let them stand without returning the fire?

The rebel lines were moving forward again. They were four hundred yards off; now three hundred. Johann could see the individual men better now. Few wore a regular uniform. Many had hats tied onto their heads by heavy scarves. Others had blankets draped about their bodies. One and all, they were thick with matted ice and snow as though they'd been out all night in the storm. Some, he saw, had no protection for their legs aside from their thick stockings. Of the mounted men, one, a tall, becloaked man, sat his horse with the ease that denoted long experience.

But just then the captain shouted, "Ready!" A pause. Then, "Aim!"

And although he hadn't been in battle since Long Island, Johann found himself going through the familiar motions automatically. The barrel of his gun wavered as he pointed it at the advancing lines.

"Fire!" roared the captain.

Johann's numbed fingers found the trigger and he pulled it. The butt slammed itself hard against his upper arm and shoulder. The shock of it only half felt, the acrid smell of gunpowder in his nose, he opened his

eyes to see the rebel lines still intact. The Hessian volley, like the rebels' had gone too high!

Now the enemy ranks were making way for the cannoneers to come forward. Shouting, they tugged at the
traces, slipped, fell, rose again. And still they came on!
And yet more men came from the woods!

Johann heard a bugle sound from behind him. The
call echoed thinly for a second or two and then was cut
off by the wind's roar.

"Back!" came the captain's command. "Fall back on
the village!"

Now Johann and his fellows slid and stumbled as
they moved eastward toward King Street and the first
houses.

"Looks to me like they got us outnumbered!" gasped
Kampel as he half slithered, half ran alongside Johann.
"But how did they ever get here over that river?"

Ahead, Johann now could see groups of Hessians
milling around the stone building that was Colonel
Rall's headquarters. Some were clustered about the cannon customarily stacked around the building. Would
they be able to get them into action in time, Johann
wondered. Men were running out of houses along the
street, buckling on belts, ramming in charges, and
clutching at flying uniforms and headpieces. A gabble
of voices and shouts was borne to the fleeing picket
guard.

Now they had almost reached the first cluster of
houses. "Quick!" ordered the captain. "In between the
houses. Use 'em as a shelter! The ranks haven't formed
yet! Hold 'em off till they get ready!"

Crouching and shivering behind a house, Johann looked out to see Americans still moving toward the junction of Pennington road and King Street at the north end of the village. While we watched, he heard another bugle call, then the rat-tat-tat of a drum. Turning, he saw that at last the von Lossberg regiment was moving out to face the enemy!

As they did so, however, the enemy's single force split, half of it moving south to form a line parallel to the row of houses behind which Johann and the picket still hid! Came a burst of musket fire, a cloud of smoke, and Johann looked out again in time to see several of the Lossbergers fall. In another minute they, too, were retreating on the village! Still the ragged cohorts poured from the woods. There must be thousands of them, Johann thought.

Now the American lines opposite the houses began to move slowly eastward, preparing to close in on the houses! Johann noticed one of the rebels stoop to re-wind a ragged piece of cloth about his bare foot. Now they were nearer! At that instant, a loud boom sounded above the wind's howl, and a heavy ball went skittering down King Street. Then, in quick succession, two more! The American artillery was in action!

He darted a quick look toward Colonel Rall's quarters, still wondering what had happened to the Hessian cannon. He saw a mounted figure ride out in front of the building. It was Colonel Rall on the chestnut!

"Where in thunder are the Knyphausens?" murmured Kampel. "They ought to have heard this an' come up to our relief."

"Hsst!" said Johann. "What's that noise?"

They listened. There it was again. A louder noise than hail. But farther away than the shots skimming up and down the streets behind them. It seemed to come from the south end of the village.

"Sounds like shootin' to me," exclaimed Kampel. "The rebels must a' come up the River Road, too. If they're down there by the Assanpink Creek bridge, then we're surrounded!"

But now there was no more time for listening or for conversation. Again the cannon at the head of King Street roared a deadly message. And simultaneously, around the corner of the house came two Americans, their weapons at the ready!

Kampel and the foremost rebel fired at the same time. Kampel's target gave a loud cry and fell. A red stain appeared on the dirty white cloth that held his hat on his head.

A buzz like an angry bee sounded close to Johann as he, too, fired. A rebel shot struck a splinter from the wall next to Johann. It went whirling off to the left. The soldier disappeared as soon as he saw he'd missed.

"Run, run! Johann, run!" It was Kampel croaking out the words. Johann turned to see him clutch his arm, stagger, then fall to the snow-covered alley between the houses.

Unheeding of the danger all about, Johann ran to kneel by Kampel's side.

"Kampel!" he shouted. "Kampel! Where are you hit?"

The eyes in the still, white face were closed. Johann

155

felt beneath the uniform for a heart beat. There was none! Kampel was dead!

It was unbelievable! The first man he had known well to be killed by a bullet after all these months! Tears rose in Johann's eyes. It seemed only minutes before when he and Kampel had been running across the snow-covered fields side by side!

A musket ball whanged close to him again. Johann started up to see a soldier duck behind the other corner of the house. Poor Kampel. There was nothing he could do for him now. To stay would be to invite certain death. Already that part of the American force that had moved on the houses along the street was going from one to the other, flushing out Hessians like so many game birds!

Glancing quickly about him, Johann saw no sign of Baum or any other picket guard member. Nor was the captain in sight. He stumbled out from the shelter of the house and ran toward a spot where he could see the colonel still astride the horse, madly waving his sword.

As he ran eastward, a bugle sounded. The signal to form up! He reached the lines just as the formation began. The colonel was shouting, "Forward, Hessians! Advance!"

All around Johann, the men in the ranks, frightened looks on every face, were grumbling and muttering. "Advance where?" murmured the nearest soldier. "They're on all sides of us!"

"He'd better move us out o' here an' fast!" rejoined another. "Their cannon can rake King or Queen Streets from one end to the other!"

At the words, two booms sounded from the head of King Street where rebel cannoneers were just barely visible. The balls came whistling down. Two Hessians were mowed down, and a third, wounded, went hopping away, screaming.

"Advance, Hessians!" came the command followed by a volley of those outlandish oaths Johann had heard so many times before.

"Advance, he's telling us," grated the same soldier. "Had he gone to his bed early last night, he'd be ready to do some advancin'. Tell me the adjutant had to wake him up; hung out the window in his nightshirt, he did yellin', 'What's the matter?' "

The words were half drowned by a renewed sound of firing from the south end of the village where the bridge crossed the creek before it swung north and to the east of where the harassed Hessians now stood. Johann wondered how the Knyphausens were faring.

But at last the cold, scared men began marching slowly east—away from the enemy's main body. The sleet beat down more fiercely than ever, stinging exposed faces and hands, sliding in icy streams down necks. Behind him Johann now heard a different booming sound.

"Must be one o' ours," said his companion. "It's about time they got those blasted things goin'."

The welcome noise of their own guns lasted but a minute or two. Then the rebels took up the refrain. One ball plowed into the retreating Hessian ranks again and took a fearful toll. Shielding his eyes against the sleet, Johann now saw the colonel loom up again.

He was almost in front of the shuffling, desperate men.

"About face, Hessians! We'll fight our way back into the village!" he roared. His voice sounded strained, different.

Stumbling, lurching, hardly aware of how they executed the familiar maneuver in the treacherous, ice-glazed snow, the ranks wheeled and started westward again.

But they had hardly taken three steps when the crash of a nearer volley rang out! Around Johann men whirled and pitched to the snow. The ugly whine of musket balls now sounded on all sides! Miraculously, mercifully, none struck him! The clouds of smoke now so mingled with the lowering storm that it was impossible to see more than a few hundred feet.

For a second time Colonel Rall came into view. But almost immediately Johann saw him, in the very act of brandishing his sword, rise higher in his stirrups, drop his weapon, and slide slowly to the ground! The chestnut went galloping away toward the creek to the rear!

How much longer it could continue this way, or how much longer he would avoid one of those singing missiles, Johann did not dare guess. Leaderless, the men had come to a halt and stood like sheep, wavering, uncertain in the wind-lashed sleet.

Out of one corner of his eye Johann saw a dull flash. He wheeled just in time to see one of the colonel's subordinates waving his hat on the tip of his sword! And in the next moment, four others followed his example, all waving their hats high above their heads!

We're going to surrender, thought Johann. What else

could their action mean? For minutes the fire did not slacken. Still the sleet pelted downward. Still the leaden hail coursed through the ranks, men dropping to the left and right!

Then out of the smoke and the storm's curtain rode an American.

"Do you surrender?" he called using the German tongue.

The officers brandished their hats on high once more. All around him, men began discarding their guns, many of them useless for the last half hour because of wet powder.

Then, miraculously the booming of cannon, the pattering and cracking of musket balls ceased. A distant crash of musketry still sounded from the south. But now, all about him, beneath the trees of the old orchard to the east of the village, only the tireless splatter of hail sounded in Johann's ears. The battle for Trenton was over!

17

CAPTIVITY AND CAMPAIGNS

COLD, hungry, and downhearted, Johann stood a few hours later, with nine-hundred-odd fellow Hessians on the snow-covered banks of the Delaware. The winter's daylight was all but gone. Sleet and snow had ended, but the cold wind sweeping down the stream sent up swells in which huge cakes of ice bobbed and wallowed.

Below, blunt-ended ungainly craft were being loaded slowly with the rebels' prisoners. Two dozen at a time, they were put into the boats, each batch guarded by half a dozen of their captors. Then the boats were poled off and carefully made their way out into the ice-packed river.

These boats, thought Johann to himself bitterly, are those we searched for not two weeks ago. He wondered where the Americans had been able to hide them to use in the dead of night for the surprise attack on Trenton.

What a complete surprise it had been! If only the picket captain had been able to read that message—the one sent by a loyalist New Jerseyman! Johann had heard about it as he trudged through the snow from Trenton to the river under guard of the triumphant Americans. The note had told of the American plans, but since it was written in English, the captain had been unable to read it!

And when Claus had brought it to Colonel Rall's headquarters, an impatient and frightened aide had barely glanced at it, then tossed it aside! But the Americans had planned the stroke well, their first decisive blow in months.

Washington had taken advantage of the widely dispersed royal armies, the impossible weather, and Colonel Rall's refusal to fortify the town, to strike shrewdly. Beginning a crossing of the river late on Christmas night, he had successfully forded it with about 2,400 men and cannon, landing on the Trenton side at about three o'clock in the morning.

The Americans had started their nine-mile march to Trenton in the same driving snow and sleet that impeded action in the battle. At a place called Birmingham, the force had been split in two, half under Washington moving to the north side of the village along the Pennington road, the other portion under the same General Sullivan once captured at Long Island moving to the south end of Trenton along the River Road. The Hessians had been trapped between the two forces. Only a few had escaped by fording the swift-running Assanpink Creek.

Colonel Rall was dead, cut down by the volley from that part of the rebel army deployed to prevent any retreat to the northeast toward Princeton. The Knyphausen regiment, surprised by Sullivan's men, had fought briefly, then surrendered too. The battle had started just after eight o'clock. Two hours later it had ended, with the captured guns stacked, and the Hessians lined up in long columns, ready for the march into captivity.

Their captors paid hardly any attention to them after the firing ceased. They went whooping through the village streets, searching for food and drink. Eventually they found it, including a large quantity of rum. To warm the half-starved, freezing men, the hogsheads had been broached.

Jugs and cups appeared as if by magic; even hats were used to get a welcome, warming taste of the raw drink. Some of the rebels, even in their moment of triumph, remembered the Hessian wounded and gave them a sip of it. While watching this scene, Johann recognized Claus among the wounded. He was lying just inside the door of a building out of the wind and the sleet.

Pretending not to understand the guard's warning to remain in line, Johann went to his side.

"Claus! Father Claus!" he cried.

The eyelids fluttered, then opened. The pale blue eyes shone with recognition, and the lips moved slightly, but no words came out.

"Are you all right? Where are you wounded?" asked Johann, seizing the cold hand and rubbing it in his own.

The American Johann had seen giving Claus some rum came near.

"Don't worry about him, Hessian," he said, not unkindly. "He's got a ball through his upper chest. He'll come around all right when we get him back to Newton across the river."

The wounded had been put aboard the boats first, then the rest of the prisoners. It seemed hours before Johann got aboard a boat—and twice as long before the narrow, pitching craft made the opposite Pennsylvania shore.

He was amazed at the way the rebels were able to carry out their job of guarding and transporting nearly a thousand prisoners. They did it with a minimum of command since few of them could speak any German. They joked among themselves, talked loudly, and laughed frequently on the tiresome march back to the river's edge.

But the tonic of victory, the first in long months, had lifted the rebels' spirits as they trudged back over the same route they'd taken only a few hours earlier. How some of them did it, Johann could hardly comprehend. Most of them were out at the elbow; few had whole

164

shoes. Some had only one, the other foot bound in cloth. They had been on the march for more than forty hours, yet few appeared to show it!

"Now maybe our esteemed Congress will feel it's safe to come back to Philadelphia," Johann heard one of the guards say to another. "They sure thought we was licked. I just wish some of them was here now."

"E-yup," replied the other. "They was quick enough to move to Baltimore when they thought the Britishers had us. But they didn't know our Gineral, did they?"

For all their seeming carelessness and merriment, the bearded, ragged men, Johann sensed, took their soldiering job with deadly seriousness. Especially when their "Gineral," a tall, blue-eyed, hawk-nosed man, wrapped closely in his cape, would from time to time ride along the straggling files.

"Take a good look at him, Hessian," called one of the guards. "He's our General. An' a better one there never was. Long live General Washington!" And his fellows, tired, cold, and hungry as they were, raised a shout that ranged up and down the line. "Long live our General!"

At the end of the march, the prisoners were herded into tents and rude huts near Newton, the rebel headquarters. Poor shelter as it was, it at least kept off the worst of the icy wind, and Johann was too tired and disheartened to do any more than fall asleep once he entered it.

A few days later the prisoners were started out under guard on the road to Philadelphia, the rebel capital. As they left the rugged, snowy countryside to enter the fringes of the settlement, Johann's nearest companion said, "Fine way to start a new year, eh, friend?"

It came as a shock to Johann to discover that nearly one year had gone by since he started out on an errand for Herr Gottfriend. Johann hadn't thought about him in a long time. Now, as he marched along, he wondered how he was, wondered, too, what had happened to Baum and Claus, or to Gorthalman. And most of all, what had happened to Ziggner and the missing watch.

Now the prisoner contingent was within the town itself. Philadelphia's streets, unlike those of New York, were wider and straighter. There were broad stone walks for pedestrians beside them. Many of the houses had awnings. It seemed a more orderly and cleaner town than New York.

The crowds that had gathered to see the first considerable batch of American captives, grew larger. It seemed everyone had come out, despite the cold. The high buildings on either side of the streets echoed and re-echoed with the cries of the onlookers and the sharper commands of the guard. Several times the latter had to push the people back on the walks to permit the prisoners to go through.

"All right! All right!" one guard cried in desperation. "You can see 'em from the sidewalk! You don't have to block the way, do you, mother?" The guard shrilled this as he hustled an elderly woman back, ignoring her protests.

The older women in the crowd seemed to take the display of prisoners more to heart than the others. Hatred flamed in their eyes. While some spectators merely gaped, scowled, or glared at the marching men in blue, the white-haired women spat in their direction or raised their skinny fists and shook them.

"Let me at 'em!" Johann heard one shriek. Tall, dressed in black, a torn cap on her head, she seemed angrier than any Johann had noticed. "Let me at 'em!" came her shout again. And before the guard could halt her, she ran into the street and clawed at Johann's face.

"You bandits!" she cried while her fingers tore at his coat, his throat, and his uniform. "Come here to rob us and our children! To stab and kill with your dirty bayonets! Too bad they didn't kill you all at Trenton!"

Surprised by the assault, Johann momentarily fell out of line. In an instant, he was surrounded by men, women, and even small boys who pummeled, pulled, and thrust at him. A sharp kick struck his shin, and, when he doubled up with the pain, a fist struck him on the head. His ears rang, and his senses began to reel.

"Death to 'em all!" the old woman was screeching.

"Kill 'em, the hired robbers!" came another roar.

But by this time, the guards had jumped into action. Dealing blows left and right with musket butts and fists, they slowly backed the angry mob toward the sidewalk. One guard grabbed Johann by the arm and pushed him into the ranks of his still-passing fellow prisoners.

Panting, scratched, his clothes ripped in half a dozen spots, Johann started to move along with the others when suddenly he saw a familiar face on the sidewalk. It was Ziggner! No doubt of it. He stood back near the building line, evidently on top of something that gave him a view over the heads of the crowds along the sidewalk.

At once Johann forgot his aches and pains, his fear of the crowd, of the guards. He leaped out of line and started to buck his way toward Ziggner, who was still looking on, but not in Johann's direction.

The sidewalk throng immediately took his wild lunge for an attempt to strike back at them, and they willingly responded. They closed around Johann again. Once more the guards hurried over, shouting and ordering the people to disperse. A fist struck Johann's jaw. Someone tripped him, and he went down. In the next instant, the mob surged over him.

It was a bruised, bleeding, and groggy Johann who was hauled to his feet by the guard. "What's the matter, Hessian?" the American soldier roared. "Think it's easier to be killed by this crowd than shot on the battlefield? Up with you an' back in them ranks. They're in no mood to be challenged this day."

"But Ziggner . . . Ziggner," moaned Johann through bruised lips. "He's . . . he's gone!"

But not all the Americans witnessing the scene were so violent, Johann saw, as the march continued, first up one street, then down another. Here and there someone tried to hand a cup of wine or a piece of bread to a prisoner. Some succeeded in this kindly gesture. But many times the proffered gift would be dashed to the street by the hands of more ill-disposed onlookers.

At last the weary parade ended, and they were ordered into a large gloomy building some distance from the center of the town. Exhausted, Johann and the others threw themselves on the hard floor. What would happen to them now? How had Ziggner managed to reach Philadelphia, Johann wondered. Did he still have the watch he had taken from Herr Crainter? And how would he, a prisoner now, ever manage to regain it?

Not many days later, one of the guards entered the long room where the Hessian prisoners stood about or lay sleeping, and began to read from a paper he held in his hand.

"The men whose names are read off, follow me to the street. You are to be moved to a more distant place of confinement."

Johann was sorry to leave. Not because he liked his cold, drafty quarters, but because he had found out by chance conversation where the Hessian wounded were. He was hopeful he could see Claus again. He had heard nothing of Baum.

The march out of town, south and east, was begun early in the day so the prisoners were not subjected again to the whim of a crowd. The few citizens who were abroad only stared silently at the lines of men as they passed.

One of their guards, more talkative than the others, proudly pointed out a building where, he announced, the Declaration of Independence had been signed but six months before. "An' they'll never take our freedom away from us now!" he declared with a scornful glance back along the prisoner ranks.

The march through the rolling countryside lasted three days. Near dusk of the last day they approached a small village. The prisoners were billeted in some rude, unoccupied buildings and locked in for the night. The next day they were told they were to remain near the village, under guard, until exchanged for an equal number of American prisoners—or until the end of the war. They were to give their word they would not attempt to escape. Captivity would be made as light as possible, and, eventually, work provided for all.

170

Johann was put in charge of one of the groups into which the whole contingent was subdivided. The duties of keeping the buildings clean, of drawing and carrying water, cutting firewood, and preparing the simple meals, were detailed to men in each squad. So at first life in the prison encampment came almost as a relief to most. As the weeks went on, though, many became bored with the monotonous existence.

But when winter gave way to the spring, a new interest sprang up. Farmers in the neighboring Pennsylvania countryside agreed to hire the prisoners as farm hands. Most took advantage of the offer as an escape from prison life. Then, as summer came on, the men were given the right to build their own, new, separate quarters. Eager hands took on this job with a will.

In a few months each of the squads had its own home. Each took pride in decorating and furnishing the log huts, each vying with the other to produce the best-appearing structure.

Meanwhile, although well behind the occurrence, news of the outside world and of the war came to the prison camp. From the lowest ebb of American fortunes, Washington had again crossed the Delaware after the first of the year and won a victory at Princeton. This triumph, once more catching the British forces napping, was followed by other harassing movements, and it brought on a general retreat of the major British and Hessian forces from New Jersey. All this within seven months after the capture of Philadelphia seemed inevitable!

Still later the prisoners heard that General Howe,

despairing of taking Philadelphia by land, had embarked his troops from Staten Island, and sailing up Delaware Bay, had landed below the city. The rebels had been defeated at the battle of Brandywine, and near the end of September, Howe entered Philadelphia.

The news caused several of Johann's companions to break parole and escape to join the victorious force. Johann had been eager to go with them, but two days before they left, to his great joy Claus was transferred from another camp.

Wan and pale, he had barely recovered from his wounds. And as much as Johann wanted to go to Philadelphia to rejoin the army, he felt he could not desert his old friend. Besides, Claus brought news that could have a bearing on the whole course of the war.

An army of more than seven thousand men under the British General John Burgoyne, Claus explained, had started south from Canada in the early summer with the grand intention of splitting the New England colonies off from the rest of the rebellious provinces.

The plan, as Claus had heard it, was that Burgoyne's army would join with one under a General St. Leger, which would march down the Mohawk Valley in York State. Taking different routes, the two bodies would move southward on Albany, and there would join with another body to be dispatched up the North or Hudson River.

But the plan had misfired. General Howe, instead of sending men north, had concentrated on his own plans to capture Philadelphia. The force coming down the Mohawk Valley had been defeated, and General Burgoyne had been left to fight it out alone! His army was harassed all the way south by the rebel woodsmen and the unexpected strength of the northern forces of the American army. He had had to surrender at Saratoga. All his force, including some Hessians, had been taken prisoner!

"And that isn't the worst of it," said Claus, as he and Johann sat at their hut door looking out at the October twilight. "The story now is that since the Americans have shown such energy in the face of odds, the French may come in on their side."

"The French?" asked Johann.

"Yes. Aye, and the Spanish, too, maybe. They would be greatly pleased to see Great Britain punished."

Claus also brought word about Baum. He had escaped with several hundred Hessians at Trenton by swimming the Assanpink Creek. When last heard of, he had joined Colonel von Donop's forces at Bordentown, but by now was probably with the army in Philadelphia.

18

ANOTHER PRISONER

THE weary months dragged on. The second winter, the most severe Johann had yet experienced, was at least spent in shelter from the incessant snow and bone-chilling cold. The British, he heard, were yet inactive in Philadelphia, making no move to join battle with the Americans only a few miles away. They were said to be freezing and starving in their own camp at a place called Valley Forge.

As did many of his fellows, Johann welcomed the advent of warmer weather and the opportunity to do some useful work at one of the nearby farms. Together with Claus and two others, Johann this year went to a new farm for the first time.

A wrinkled, nearsighted American farmer greeted them at the boundary of his pasture. Yes, he told the guard, he'd wanted some "Heshians" to work for him, heard they were good farmers. Within a week's time the four soldiers were on as friendly terms with their rebel masters as they had been with the others for whom they'd worked. The Americans were easy to get along with, Johann found, once you allowed for the way they talked.

The food, too, was no slight attraction for the hard, daylong labor in the fields. Despite the demands of the local militia and occasional forays of the American regulars, there always seemed to be plenty of meat, milk, and eggs on the table. Johann became the special pride of the farmer's grandson, Tom, a boy of about eight.

One day at the dinner table, young Tom boasted:

"We'll soon have Uncle Zack home, won't we, Gran'pa?"

The old man smiled at the boy's enthusiasm, then explained in carefully chosen words what he meant:

"You see, my brother's boy, Zack, he's just been released as a prisoner of the British in New York. Captured at the battle of Fort Washington." He paused, then asked as though suddenly remembering, "Any o' you fellers fit there?"

The name "Zack" had a familiar ring to Johann. He thought for a moment—then it came to him! Could this Zack be the rebel boy he had had the fight with in the hill fort? Eagerly, he pressed the old man for a description of his nephew. Was he brown-haired, slight, with a freckled face?

"That's him, all right," beamed the farmer. "Where'd you see him last?"

For a minute, Johann hardly knew how to say it in his halting English. He feared he would offend the old man by his description of that defeat. But as all at the table began to stare at him, Johann decided to tell his story.

The farmer listened in silence. Young Tom, eyes starting, listened quietly, too, while Johann told how the Americans, hemmed in by superior force, unable to be evacuated as originally planned, had given up the fight. And finally, how Zack had shaken his hand as he marched off a prisoner.

"Well, that does beat all," finally remarked the old man. "To think you knowed my Zack." Then he brightened. "He'll be here in a couple o' days. You fellers can swap stories." Then he started to laugh. "He was right though, wasn't he?" he asked. "He said we'd get our turn, an' we did. Why, they tell me the same flags you fellers took from our side at that fight was taken back agin at Trenton."

The farmer's information turned out to be true. Zack did come home. But it was an older, sadder Zack than Johann remembered. The thin frame if anything was even thinner. Gone were the freckles, replaced by a pallor that not even the hot summer's sun could relieve. He walked with a limp, a cane in one hand.

But when the old man broke the news to him about

the new "hired hands," and he came slowly through the ripening corn to the place where Johann, Claus, and the others were hard at work, there could be no doubting who he was. For once more the right hand came out. A twisted, shrunken hand, it was true, but a hand. And a thin voice said:

"Well, Heshian. I guess we're even now, ain't we?"

It was hard to believe his story. Zack and the thousands of others captured at Fort Washington had been moved almost at once to the prison ships anchored off New York. And there they had lain, dying by the hundreds, ill-fed, ill-treated, until the day came when Zack was released.

Recounting his experiences in more detail later, as they sat on the bench beside the well, Zack told Johann:

"That's why your side ain't goin' to win. You can't treat humans like that an' expect they're goin' to like you. That's been the trouble right along. The Britishers thought jest 'cause we are a bunch o' farmers, they could rule us an' make us like it. But we didn't, an' we tol' 'em. They didn't believe it, an' sent soldiers over here to scare us into likin' it. But we don't scare that easy."

Zack brought news, too. General Howe had resigned. The British had evacuated Philadelphia and returned to New York!

"An' the Frenchies hev signed a treaty o' assistance with us," he commented. "An' when that Frenchy fleet gets over here, you fellers won't be able to do so good, I'm thinkin'."

On another day, after Zack got stronger and was helping with the work, he asked Johann:

"What for are you Heshians in this anyways? 'Tain't any o' your fight."

Johann told briefly how he had been "recruited" for fighting with the British forces. Zack was silent for a few moments after he heard the story.

"So's you really ain't got any interest in this here fight between us an' the Britishers, hev' you?"

Johann thought hard for a moment. He had to admit that Zack had a point. He and his friends, it suddenly struck him, were only fighting because they had been "hired out" by their ruler, the Landgrave.

"The men of Hesse-Cassel have always been good soldiers," he replied stiffly. "They always obey orders. When they're told to fight, they do it. And well—as you know."

"But what," cried Zack, "hev you, fer instance, agin me? Agin Uncle? Or Tommy? We're only tryin' to per-tect our country. Can't you see that?"

Sleep was long in coming to Johann that night. As he tossed, he turned Zack's words over and over in his mind. Would these people, with so little in the way of an army, be so willing to fight if they didn't have some strong belief in their cause?

Was it so wrong, Johann pondered, to fight because he had been hired to do so? After all, Hessians had done it for centuries. Then he thought of the old farmer, of Zack, of the boy, Tommy. Their faces moved slowly in his thoughts. Honest, cheerful, friendly faces. Could they be wrong? He fell asleep still thinking about it.

A few days later, Johann was given more food for

thought, when Zack again opened the subject of fighting for one's country or for someone else by saying:

"I tell you, you ain't goin' to get the upper hand. Wait an' see. The Britishers an' you fellers has had all the advantages so far—men, money, ships. But yet you ain't won, an' the war's been goin' on fer years. You know, Heshian, I like you. Why'n't you stay here with us? All you got to do is give up your allegiance. You'll find we ain't hard folk to get on with. An' believe me, when this here war's over, you'll really see somethin' of this country. Why they's miles o' it nobody's ever seen yet. Room for everyone."

But somehow, Johann—and Claus, too, who heard part of Zack's plea—couldn't forsake their fellow soldiers. They thanked Zack and his uncle when the summer ended, and went back to the encampment, brown, well-fed, a small sum of money in their pockets, and regretful that they had to leave the pleasant Pennsylvania farm. As they trudged down the road the last day, Johann found himself wondering whether Zack might be right. Could it be that the righteous will of these farmers would, in the end, triumph over the trained armies of the King and the Landgrave?

Johann and the others had almost given up hope of ever returning to their commands, when, in the third spring of their imprisonment, the welcome word came that they had been exchanged for an equal number of American prisoners. Johann, who had not worked for Zack's uncle that summer, received permission to go to the farm to say good-by.

179

Zack's face lighted up when he saw the Hessian approach.

"Ain't seen you since last year," he greeted. "How you been?" Zack looked rested. He had more color in his face after a season in the open. He insisted that Johann enter the house to have a cooling drink of milk and some warm, fresh bread. When he heard the news, his face shaded slightly.

"I'm sorry to hear that, Heshian," he said shortly. "But ef'n you feel you'll do better with your friends— why that's up to you." He paused, extended his hand, and shook Johann's warmly. "But remember what I tol' you. We're goin' to win. An' ef'n you don't want to be on the losin' side, best get off it soon!" Both laughed, then Johann turned and left the farm for the last time.

Back at the camp the joy at the news of the exchange still ran high. Men danced about in the space before the huts, shouted, and slapped each other on the back. Some were even beginning to pack, as though they meant to leave that very afternoon.

"Almost seems too good to be true," mused Johann out loud to Claus as they watched the scene.

"It may be too true to be good," somberly replied Claus.

Two days later they were marched to the nearest port and began the long voyage to New York and the army from which they had been separated for three long years.

19

A JOURNEY TO THE UNKNOWN

IT seemed good to Johann to be back in New York again, to walk along the familiar streets, to smell the salt air, and particularly to walk along the docks on off-duty hours and watch the busy shipping in the North River.

More pleasant yet was it to have Baum and Father Claus walking with him. Johann and Claus had hardly arrived in the town when they encountered Baum, haggling as usual with a native for a basket of fruit. The reunion was as noisy as it was unexpected.

Baum, they learned, had rejoined the remnants of the regiment that fled from Trenton, and had fought without a scratch through all the ensuing campaigns, from the Delaware up to Sandy Hook, and back again to Philadelphia. Then, retracing his steps, he returned to New York.

He and a number of Hessians had narrowly escaped capture a few months before when an expedition under the American General Harry Lee had surprised the fortifications at Paulus Hook opposite New York.

"But for the past three months we been cooped up here, with little to do," recounted Baum. "The British-ers have been tryin' to get up the North River to the fortifications at West Point. They took, then lost, then recaptured Stony Point up the river about thirty-five miles. But from here on, believe me, the story is goin' to be different, 'specially since the French fleet has been sailin' up an' down the coast an' nobody knows where it will show next."

But Johann hardly heard what he said, for, just at that moment a man came running from the door of a shop just ahead. Right behind the first man, a second, apron flapping, came hurrying to the street.

"Stop, thief! Stop!" Johann heard the second man call.

Johann, Baum, and Claus broke into a run behind the shopkeeper. But the man ahead picked up speed and darted down an alley toward Whitehall Slip. The shopkeeper's cries and the clatter of boots on the pave-ment all attracted instant attention, and in a minute Johann found himself and his companions part of a running, panting throng, all crying, "Stop, thief!" at the top of their lungs.

"Fellow looks like someone I know," gasped Johann to Claus as they dodged around a cart that blocked the narrow street.

"He can't go much farther," grunted Baum, matching step for step for all his greater years. "This street lets out on the water front. If he's to escape us, he'll have to swim for it."

The buildings echoed with the uproar now. Men at work, shopkeepers, carters, small boys, and not a few soldiers, attracted by the commotion, joined in the pursuit. Around the corner at the end of the street the crowd dodged, just in time to see the man they were chasing run out on a stringpiece, pause a moment, then leap into a small boat.

"Curse the luck," exclaimed Baum when, puffing loudly, he and the others reached the shore. "No other boat in sight, and, say, look at him row, will you?"

The shopkeeper, an elderly man, continued to shout, "Stop, thief!" as the boat was dexterously maneuvered around one vessel after another and out toward midstream.

"What did he take from you?" asked Johann.

"He said he wanted to get a greatcoat," mumbled the old man, his thinning gray hair spilling down over his leathery face in the strong river breeze. "Said he'd give me a watch in trade for it. Then . . . when I agreed to give him some money for the watch over the greatcoat's cost, he seized the money—and the watch—and ran out!

183

The dirty thief!" And he raised his voice again: "Stop, thief!"

But the man in the boat was plying the oars industriously, back and head bowed in the effort. As he neared another of the moored ships, he raised his head to glance backwards for his bearings. And at that moment, Johann saw his face. It was Ziggner! So, he thought, if the old shopkeeper is right, Ziggner still has the watch!

"Did you look inside the watch case?" Johann asked eagerly.

"That I did. I'm not buying any broken timepieces. Lord only knows there are enough bad ones in New York these days," replied the old man.

"Did it have anything inside it?" asked Johann.

"Naught unusual," the man replied. Then, as Johann's heart sank, he added, "Unless it was the scratchings on the inside of the case."

But by this time the boat was well out in the river in the shadows cast by the river's westerly cliffs, or "Palisades," as they were called, apparently headed for the New Jersey shore.

As Johann, the shopkeeper, and the others turned from the quay, still discussing the chase and Ziggner's escape, the small boat in which he had fled was just rounding the stern of a brig, the *Triton,* anchored well out. Unseen at that distance by those on shore, Ziggner grasped a line that trailed from the vessel, and slowly, hand over hand, began to hoist himself to the deserted deck above.

Not long after this the routine of the daily roll call was enlivened when the officer in charge read off the orders of the day:

"At ten o'clock in the forenoon tomorrow, September eighth, the following-named members of this brigade will report, with gear in order, at the quayside, prepared to embark for service at a destination as yet unannounced."

The order was enough to set a flood of rumor seething in the ranks of the Regiments von Lossberg and von Knyphausen, the latter the one to which Johann and Claus had been assigned on their return to New York. Were they going southward where, according to all reports, the main theater of the war would shortly open? Or would they head for Halifax? Most exciting of all, and here rumor only whispered the hope, would it be for home?

The day dawned red and threatening. The smell of rain was in the air as the men, marching in time to fife and drum, went to the water front. At an officer's direction, Johann's company and one other were directed to board a small brig that heaved and rocked at its dock in the rising swells. As he followed Baum up the gangway, Johann noticed the ship's name, *Triton*, etched in faded letters on her bow.

"Wonder how long she's been knockin' around," muttered Baum when they reached the dirty, well-worn deck. "I just hope we're not goin' far in this tub. It don't look to me like she's long for this world."

Even an unpracticed Johann and Claus were inclined to agree with the old soldier after they had been shown to the dirty, smelly hold. It was almost as crowded as the transport had been, with men and gear hopelessly intermingled in the gloomy 'tween decks.

Back on topside for a welcome breath of fresh air, Johann and Baum took a turn around the cluttered deck. Although the *Triton* was already low in the water, a large number of boxes and bales were piled high aft. The few crewmen visible, hurrying to cast her off, were hardly helped by the obstructions.

At last the ship drew away from shore, dropped through the Narrows, and so, down the Lower Bay into the open sea. As the last of the green hills faded from sight, Johann wondered whether he'd ever see New York again. The trip across the ocean had been difficult, the heat, the snows, the battles had not been lightly borne, yet he felt there was something about the town and the country he liked.

Again he wondered what had happened to Ziggner. Did he still have the watch? Or maybe—Johann trembled at that thought—maybe he's sold it by now!

By the next morning the promise of stormy weather had come true. The seas were mounting, their white-crested tops rolling in an ever moving procession from the north. As the tremendous walls of green bore down on the *Triton,* it seemed they must engulf her. But somehow, deep-laden as she was, she rose over every one and plunged on.

As Johann watched this awesome scene, a whistle shrilled somewhere up forward. Then he heard shouts, but because of the wind's noise, could not make out what was said. As he looked about, a few of the ship's

186

crewmen ran to the vessel's six small cannon and began loading them.

Baum came running up, followed by Claus, both lurching and swaying against the movement of the ship.

"Sail's been sighted to the west," rasped Baum. "The ship's captain thinks it may be an American privateer from Little Egg Harbor."

Johann had heard of this port where American privateersmen gathered to make periodic raids on British ships entering or leaving New York harbor.

Johann was amazed at the way the brown, half-naked sailors readied the guns while the deck beneath them rolled and pitched. Then, as he watched, the sails of a larger vessel loomed over the horizon. It came nearer until Johann could plainly see the mountain of canvas under which it fairly tore across the waves. The ship's captain, glass in hand, waved his free hand. The gunners lit their matches and prepared to fire the cannon on the port side, as well as the swivel gun on the bow.

Then, over the howling of the wind in the rigging, Johann heard the captain shout:

"Belay it. She's friendly. She's a British transport."

Twenty minutes later, the huge transport, lines and canvas crackling as she executed the maneuver, towered alongside the *Triton*.

"His Majesty's transport *Alexander*," came the cry through the speaking trumpet from the other ship. "Who are you?"

Now Johann saw the ship's captain conferring with Captain Kelle, in charge of the soldiers aboard. Then he heard the answering hail:

"Brig *Triton* with two regiments of soldiers of the Landgrave of Hesse-Cassel aboard."

"Where are you bound?" came the question.

"We're under sealed orders," roared back the *Triton*'s captain. "We were supposed to rendezvous with a fleet tomorrow."

"Sealed orders," muttered Baum in Johann's ear. "That could mean anything—or nothing. We'll see what happens next."

The next order relayed commanded the *Triton* to follow the transport back toward New York. With a shrilling of pipes and movement of the crew about the lines, the big ship wheeled slowly and set off westward, the *Triton* riding like a small, wallowing duck in her wake.

Shortly after noon on the next day, Johann saw sail after sail fairly pop up over the horizon. He counted twenty-five all together, all about the same size as the *Alexander* save two. These, as they came closer, turned out to be armed barks, convoying the fleet.

As the *Triton* and *Alexander* neared, a flurry of signals broke from the armed ships, and were repeated from all of the transports Johann could see.

"Still looks to me as though we were headed for the south—maybe Charleston in the Carolinas," said Baum. "Heard they've been doin' a lot of fightin' down there of late." He sighed. "An' I thought maybe we'd get out of it. Ha!" And he spat over the side in disgust.

For the next two days the voyage continued without event, the *Triton,* for all her size, keeping up with the bigger ships. She did it, however, only because, at Captain Kelle's orders, two seamen were transferred from one of the transports to aid in working the badly under-manned brig.

On the third day, however, the storm that had first plagued them, seemed to return, the wind rising by the hour.

By the following day it became so strong that two sails were blown clean out of their ropes, and, until the remainder were close-hauled, the brig seemed in danger of losing all way. The rain now was driving in sheets. With every lurch forward, the huge waves battered at the *Triton*'s blunt bow, burying it beneath tons of water.

Visibility was cut to a few hundred yards of dirty, angry, gray waves that slashed forward at racing speed. In the curtain of wind-blown rain, the rest of the convoy was quickly lost to sight.

Seated below in his crowded quarters that night, Johann munched away at an apple he'd been able to find in the provision barrel. The creaking and wrack-ing of the timbers about and above him were terrific. Each time a wave struck, the ship's whole frame shud-dered and shook. The feeble light from the lamp amid-ships had long since burned out. But Johann could hear the moans and cries of his fellows, made ill by the vio-lent pitching of the *Triton* and, like himself, fearful for their fate.

If I stay down here much longer, he thought, I'll get ill, too. He had just risen to his feet, called to Baum and Claus nearby that he was going above, when a loud cracking sound came from on deck. Then, with a noise that made his ears sing, something heavy fell! The vessel shook from stem to stern!

Scrambling to his feet, Johann sensed that Baum and Claus were at his side.

"Sounds like she lost a mast!" roared Baum. "Let's get up on deck while the chance is good!"

Stumbling over men and gear, bounced like corks against the bulkheads, the three groped their way to the hatch ladder. As Johann poked his head out to be slapped in the face with a stinging shower of rain and salt water, he heard further creaking sounds. They were quickly followed by another deafening crash.

One behind the other, they crept along the deck, clinging to a life line strung on the starboard side. But they had not gone far when Johann crawled into a tangle of ropes and lines, into a smother of wet, flapping canvas.

"Must be her mizzenmast," shouted Baum. "We won't live ten minutes in this storm with the wreckage draggin'. Come with me."

Despite the darkness and the obstacles, the three made their way aft where already some of the crew, judging by the sharp-sounding strokes of axes, were trying to clear the ship. In the feeble, flickering light of a dark lantern held beneath a coat to protect it against the wind, two crewmen, barely able to see what they were doing, chopped for dear life. When at last it was entirely free, the sailors, helped by the three soldiers, heaved it overboard.

"Quick, to the foremast now!" called the ship's captain. "Lively, or we're lost!"

Again the stumbling and lurching water-drenched passage over the quaking deck. Again, the strokes of axes directed more by instinct than sight. And once more the heaving, straining lift on the slippery mast in a desperate race with time and the storm! At last it was cleared!

Now without its masts, the *Triton* yawed and pitched even more fearsomely. At one moment Johann felt he must fall backward against the nearest bulkhead; at the next he felt he would pitch headlong down the wave-drenched deck into the sea! Huge, wall-like combers, their dark tips faintly lit with spray, roared out of the night to strike the vessel, broke, then poured over her decks.

Winded, spent, and drenched, Johann clung to the line amidships. Suddenly he heard a noise that surmounted the storm's roar. It was a rolling, hollow sound that seemed to come from nowhere—yet from everywhere. What could it be?

Then he heard a faint hail:

"Ahoy, the bridge! The cannon are sprung from their lashings!"

AN ENEMY'S RETURN

NOW the rolling, hollow noise sounded closer. Something huge and black, something undeterred by the waves, with spray breaking over it, passed the three huddling in the dark. The deck shivered beneath the rasping, rumbling roar of tons of iron propelled, directionless, about the heaving ship. With a splintering of wood it struck the bulwarks not five feet from where Johann clutched his line, and disappeared in a smother of froth over the side!

"Destination unknown," howled Baum. "That was as

true a description of us as ever I heard. We'll be at the bottom in no time unless those guns are secured."

And, as though to emphasize his words, the angry sea, lifting again, screeched through the rent the cannon had made. Gasping, choking for breath, Johann raised himself higher on his line.

"Here comes another," screamed Claus. And in a minute, while they prayed it would miss them, a second iron monster charged down the deck, struck savagely at the bulwark, bounded back, and then went careening off into the bow. Johann heard another grating and creaking of wood.

"There goes number two!" called Baum. "Let's get out of here before we're flattened by the next one."

Holding on to each other with one hand, clinging to the lines with the other, they managed to reach the hatch once more. Only Baum's sharp eyesight guided them in the crashing, pitching dark.

For a minute after getting out of the spray and the wind, Johann felt safer. But the next moment as he heard the hollow rattling of the other cannon on the deck above, listened to the creaking of the ship and the groans of the men in the hold, he was almost willing to go back on deck.

Over his head he heard the rolling of wheels end in a loud clanging burst of sound, to be instantly followed by the violent smashing of wood. "There goes a third," muttered Claus. "Sounds like our mess kettle must have gone with it. God send the others follow it."

But even as he spoke, a crescendo of rolling wheels ended in a sickening splintering of wood. Johann felt himself propelled violently backward, struck his head on the bulkhead, and lost consciousness.

He came to himself to hear the vessel still creaking, still groaning, still pitching. Hardly knowing what to expect, he felt himself cautiously. Something slithered under his hand. Something wet. Slippery.

"Help!" he croaked. "Help me, Baum!"

There was no answer. Nothing but the sound of the storm, the groans of the sick men about him. Then, miraculously, a light shone in his face, and, looking down at him, face a-grin, stood Baum.

"All right, lad?" he yelled. "I pulled you back just in time. But you'll have to go up on deck again to wash that uniform off, I guess."

"What do you mean?" asked Johann. "Am I hurt that bad?"

"Nothin' that a good sea won't help," Baum laughed. "Come on, lad. Get up. You're all right. Come with me, I want to show you somethin'."

Still wondering why he felt no broken bones, Johann rose slowly, bracing himself against the ship's plunges.

"Look," said Baum. "Look down there."

Holding the light above him, Baum pointed downward to the hold below. There, its muzzle still pointed upward, was one of the loosened cannon! It had plunged through a hatch, by some miracle missed the men lying on either side, and then fallen into a huge provision chest.

"You're covered with the finest mixture of wine, vinegar, and mustard that ever graced any tavern's table," said Baum. "The gun smashed it wide open and scattered the stuff all about the hold. Smell it?"

Johann trembled when he considered his narrow escape. But for Baum's timely shove, he would have been right in the gun's downward path! Then, as he sniffed the aromatic air, he began to laugh.

On deck now, the rolling noises had ceased. But there was still no lessening of the storm's sounds. At that moment one of Captain Kelle's aides, lantern in hand, peered down through the broken hatch.

"Hey, down there!" he called. "Anyone alive? Those who are and call themselves true Hessians, come on deck at once! We need your help! Quick, now!"

Once more Johann climbed to the deck. Baum was right behind him, followed by Claus and only a pitiful half-dozen of men able to rise from their sickbeds.

At the stump of the foremast the ship's captain and Captain Kelle were gathered. "You men there," shouted Captain Kelle, "bear a hand with this pump. There aren't enough seamen to man it and work the ship, too! If you value your worthless skins, the pump must be put to work! She's taking water aft! Quick! To it!"

Hardly knowing what he was to do or how, Johann grabbed the pump handle with Claus and Baum and began moving it up and down. Up and down. Up and down. While the rain streamed with renewed force, the ship threatened at any moment to succumb to the battering waves.

Gasping, drawing in spray with every other breath, Johann labored as he never had before.

"Keep at it, men!" encouraged the ship's captain. "We're not taking any more water. Keep it up!"

"Faster! Faster!" roared Captain Kelle.

Mechanically now, eyes shut against the flying spume, legs aching, and arms nearly numb, Johann kept at it. Up and down. Then, suddenly, when it seemed he had spent hours at the task, Johann felt the handle's motion slow, then stop! Baum's voice sounded in his ear: "Let go, lad. Let go. 'Tis no use. It won't work any more."

Too tired to care, Johann felt himself slip to the wet deck. But in an instant he was up again. The pump not working? What would happen to them now?

With a desperation born of despair, he grabbed at the pump handle again, pulled on it. But it stayed down at the end of the stroke. It was only then he realized the sailors, too, had ceased their efforts!

His new-found strength ebbed then, and Johann once more dropped to the deck, oblivious of the spray and the danger of being rolled or washed overboard. He wished the *Triton* would go down soon. Anything would be better, he thought, than the endless battering, the cold, and the horrible pitching of the leaking, helpless craft.

Lying in the blackness, he wondered where the others had gone, hearing no voices about him. He raised himself on one elbow and noticed a faint glimmer of light somewhere up forward. A group of men had gathered about one of the ship's small boats.

Fear swept over him. Were they going to abandon the ship? Would he be left behind to die? Where were Baum and Claus? Shielding his eyes against the flying water, Johann raised himself to his feet, swaying and rolling with the ship's motion.

He had taken one, then two, uncertain steps toward the men at the bow when his ears caught the noise of a hatch cover violently opened behind him. At the same time another light flickered from somewhere in back.

He turned to see a single figure lurch across the deck to the bulwark. The lantern the man carried shed its light on the nearest boat swaying in the lines that held it to the davits. In the next instant the man climbed into the boat!

Unbelieving, Johann saw him busy himself about the davits, the light bobbing in the gale, the boat swinging pendulumlike with the ship's every movement. The man set the light down on a thwart to seize the lowering line, and in that moment Johann saw his face! It was Ziggner!

Releasing his hold on the life line, Johann fairly threw himself across the slippery deck. With a shock that almost knocked the wind out of him, he crashed into the bulwarks, right beside the boat!

The creaking of the blocks told him that Ziggner was starting to lower away! There was no time to lose!

"Ziggner!" he shouted, his words whipped away by the wind. "Ziggner! Stop!"

Slowly, canting first to one side then the other, the boat began to fall below the deck, nearer and nearer the raging waves and their rugged crests, now running almost level with the deck!

For an instant Ziggner, his face glowering in the

light, looked straight at Johann, then in the next second the boat struck the water. Once, it heaved up, miraculously afloat; in the next moment it dipped into a trough, crunched against the ship's side, rose again!

Helplessly, Johann watched while Ziggner unshipped an oar and tried to fend the craft off. At the same moment he saw the men at the bow start to run toward him!

The wind whipping at his spray-soaked clothes, but choosing his hold with care, Johann climbed to the bulwarks, paused a moment, then jumped—far out, arms flailing above his head!

Even in mid-air, glancing downward, he saw the bobbing boat rise toward him! He landed feet first near the stern, his leap perfectly timed! The plunging motion of the cockleshell craft made him almost lose his balance, but he saved himself from going into the sea by seizing the gunwale!

Ziggner was now trying to use his single oar. But in that sea the effort was unavailing! The boat spun and rocked wildly, still only feet away from the ship, at every minute threatening to crunch like an eggshell against the *Triton*'s side.

Turning, Ziggner for the first time realized Johann was in the boat with him. His features streaming water, his hair matted against his head, Ziggner rose from the bow where he had been kneeling and moved cautiously toward the lad! He clutched the boat's side to steady himself with one hand, while with the other he held tightly to the oar.

"The milksop clerk again!" he shouted, the hatred in

his eyes gleaming in the light's rays. "We meet once more, eh? Well, it won't be me this time." Now he raised himself erect, clutched the oar in both hands and slowly lifted it above his head. As he did so, the boat spun crazily and the light fell into the raging sea!

Fearful now that if he loosened his own hold, he would plunge in after it, Johann could but sit motionless, silent, awaiting the descent of the heavy wooden blade! He closed his eyes, and, as he did, the recollection of that fight with Hantzle somehow flashed through his mind! In the next instant, fears forgotten, Johann lunged through the darkness, ducked inside the outspread arms, and seized Ziggner around the waist.

For a second too surprised to let go the oar, Ziggner, outweighing Johann by many pounds, was locked in his desperate embrace! The two swayed with the boat's motion. Then Ziggner dropped the oar! The brawny arms drew in and big hairy hands clutched at Johann's throat. Johann held on, weaving and shifting with every jerk of the boat and of Ziggner's big body.

Johann felt himself slowly forced backward until he lay almost flat in the sloshing water at the boat's bottom. Still the pressure tightened on his throat. Breath coming in gasps, Johann suddenly shifted his hold and grasped one of Ziggner's arms. He must tear away that strangling hold! Another sickening roll of the boat and Johann's head hit one of its strakes. He hung on to the forearm of his foe, but he felt his strength begin to fail. Then the boat gave a sudden wild dip astern and to starboard! In the next instant Ziggner lost his hold on Johann, flew over the boy's head, and pitched into the sea!

Breathless, Johann lay in the bottom of the boat, rolling from side to side with its every motion. When he raised himself to his knees, Ziggner had disappeared! Only the empty, crested, hissing waves rolled by, snatching at the frail boat with wet, hungry reaches.

Johann turned to look for the ship. It was still only yards away, its dark bulk rising and falling in the half-light that marked the onset of day. A lantern was shining from somewhere near midships.

At a faintly heard hail, Johann looked up to see someone on board brandishing a coil of rope. And in the next minute the heavy, leaded end landed in the boat's bottom. Scrabbling forward, Johann grabbed, missed, then grabbed it again just before the end slid out of the boat. It was a second's work to fasten it securely.

Now, thought Johann, she'll be smashed against the side of the ship! Already well filled with water, the boat was sinking lower and lower. A second line came over, and he heard Baum's voice rasp over the tumult:

"Tie it around you! We'll haul you in! Never mind the boat!"

Quickly, Johann stood up. He made one knot around his body and another. Then his stocking foot felt something in the bottom of the boat. Something hard and round. Forgetting the dangers of being splintered against the *Triton*, forgetting the wildly pitching boat and the shrieking hurricane, he stooped down, feeling elbow-deep in the cold water.

His hand groped again. There! There it was! He clutched the object and drew it out of the water. It was a watch! It must be his father's watch! But just then the line about him tightened. He felt himself drawn upward, swinging like a top, banging against the planks of the ship. Up and up, half smothered in the waves, until at last he lay, just as he had that long-ago day at the school playground, surrounded by dimly seen boots and legs. Then he knew no more.

21

A RESOLUTION

BAUM was the first person Johann saw when he opened his eyes again. It was strangely quiet now. The dreadful creaking and wrenching of the ship's timbers had subsided to a more rhythmic sound.

Johann sat upright in his rude berth as recollection flooded over him.

"Baum! Baum!" he called. "Where's the watch?"

His old friend's features crinkled in a warm smile as he looked up from some papers he held in his hand.

"Oho, lad. A tough one you are," said Baum. "Feelin' better, eh?"

"Never mind that," interposed Johann. "What happened to my watch?"

"There, there, lad. Don't fret yourself. I have it right with me." And he held up the battered watch by its short chain. Its surface caught the light as it swung slowly around in Baum's hand. Johann thought he'd never seen a more lovely sight.

"Give it to me. I can hardly believe I have it at last!" murmured Johann. "But tell me, what happened?"

Baum then explained that Captain Kelle had suspected the ship's captain of trying to launch the boats and put off with the crew, leaving the ill and exhausted soldiers to the mercy of the storm.

"But as God would have it," Baum said, "the captain, Claus, and I caught him inspectin' the boats. Captain Kelle accused him of plottin' to abandon ship, but he denied it. However, it didn't do him no good, 'cause while Claus grabbed his lantern, the captain and I grabbed him."

"Captain Kelle placed him under arrest, an' me and Claus was takin' him to his cabin when we seen the light at the other end o' the ship. We seen the boat launched, then somebody—we didn't know it was you then—leap into it."

"We thought you was a gone goose, specially when we realized Ziggner was in the boat with you an' seen him raise that oar. . . ."

"Did . . . did," broke in Johann, "you ever see more of him after . . . after he fell out of the boat?"

"We never seen him again. An' besides, we was too busy tryin' to figure out some way o' bringin' you back to us. You can thank Claus's strong right arm for those two lines he heaved."

"What happened to the boat?" asked Johann.

"It filled an' sank the minute we landed you. It was probably just as rotten as the others we found by daylight this mornin'. None o' them were fit to put to sea in, so's we cut 'em all loose. What madness the sea captain an' his men were thinkin' o', I can't imagine." He paused, then added, "But right now they're workin' the pump for dear life. They managed to fix it when day broke. It may be we'll still stay on top—for awhile at least."

"But the watch, Baum," cried Johann. "You haven't given me the watch." And he reached out for it.

"That I didn't," chuckled Baum. "But it hardly seems worth all the trouble you went through to get it. Why, it don't even run. I know you told me how it belonged to your father an' that you wanted to get it back —but what good's a battered turnip like that?"

"I'll show you," said Johann, trembling as he felt the watch once more in his hands. He pressed the hinge, and the stained back opened slowly. There it was inside, a crudely drawn map, etched on the case, with the scrawled words beneath: "To Wilhelm Leonhardt, for his heirs and assigns." And beneath, small, almost indecipherable, the name, "Josias Robbinson, 1774."

"But what does that mean? I looked at that," said Baum, screwing up his eyes to see the fine lines, "but it don't mean nothin' to me. Does it to you?"

"It means everything to me," slowly answered Johann, glancing long and lovingly at the watch and its scratches. "This proves to me that my father did, as Herr Gottfriend told me, receive a deed of the property inscribed in this watch from his friend, the sea captain, Robbinson." He paused. Overhead he could hear the pump steadily sucking away. "It means I'm no longer a penniless orphan." He halted again, then added softly, "Thanks to you and Claus."

But Baum was no longer looking at the watch or at Johann. Instead, he picked up the paper he had been looking at.

"Then this," the words stumbled over one another, "is yours, too, lad."

"What is it, Baum?" asked Johann as he looked at the closely scribbled writing. "What makes you think it's mine? Where did you find it?"

" 'Tis a long story, lad. But, briefly, after we pulled you aboard the *Triton,* we noticed one o' the messmen cringin' on the deck behind us. His curiosity about Ziggner's fate led us to question him. First off, he claimed to know nothin'.

"Then, when we pressed him, Brante—that was his name—confessed he'd known Ziggner when both o' them was members o' a lawless band that preyed on innocent folk in the countryside round Harlem an' in Westchester County nearby. . . ."

"The outlaws!" exclaimed Johann, remembering the incident at the Liberty Tree Tavern.

"Yes," replied Baum, "that's what he called 'em. He told us Ziggner was one o' the leaders o' the band. After the campaign moved to New Jersey an' the Delaware, Ziggner, he said, mysteriously disappeared. Brante says he suspects Ziggner betrayed 'em afore he dropped out o' sight. The rebels later captured most o' the gang an' hung not a few."

"What else did he say about Ziggner?" asked Johann. "And what has this story to do with the paper you just gave me?"

"Wait, wait a bit, lad," answered Baum. "I'm gettin' to that. This Brante was one o' them what escaped. He went to New York an' signed up with the *Triton*. He made several voyages on her atween New York an' Halifax.

"To make a long story short, when the *Triton* was last in port, Brante ran into Ziggner. That scum threatened to tell on him unless he agreed to take him aboard the ship. Ziggner, it appears, was playin' both ends against the middle, joinin' up with either the British or the Americans as fortune seemed best suited. He told Brante a rebel agent was on his track, an' he had to leave New York for awhile."

"Go on! Go on!" said Johann.

"Well, the day you an' me an' Claus chased him, the day he rowed away in the boat, he got on board the *Triton*. When she put to sea, he showed himself to Brante an' demanded he be kept hid till the ship reached its next port."

"But where does this paper come into the story?" asked Johann.

"I'm comin' to that," replied the other. "Brante hid Ziggner in a cubby aft. One day when Brante surprised him readin' the paper an' asked what it was, Ziggner just laughed an' said, 'If I ever get back to the old country, my fortune's made.' But that's all he said. After we questioned Brante, he led us to the hidin' place, an' we found this paper stuffed beneath a loose board.

"The way I figger it, Ziggner didn't intend leavin' it behind. He must a' gone on deck 'cause he was frightened by the storm, seen how low the *Triton* lay in the water, didn't see anyone around, an' feared she'd been abandoned. So he tried to escape in the boat."

"But you still haven't said why this paper concerns me," impatiently interposed Johann.

"Here. Give it back," answered Baum. Then, holding it up to get a better look at the crabbed writing, he slowly read:

"In the name of God, amen. I, Wilhelm Leonhardt, being of sound mind, and wishing to meet Divine Providence with a clear conscience, declare this to be my last will and testament. I give and bequeath to my only son, Johann Leonhardt, of Cassel, all my worldly goods now held in the vaults of Herr Crainter at Number 3, Water Street, in the town of New York. I further give and bequeath to Herr Crainter one (1) gold watch as given me by my friend Captain Josias Robbinson, to be held by said Crainter until my said son Johann shall claim it. And I do further declare the map of property, which property was given me by said Robbinson, inscribed on the back of the watch case, is to be the property of my son, Johann."

Baum handed the paper back and asked gently:

"Do you recognize the signature?"

Through dimming eyes, Johann looked at the writing. There was no doubt of it. The paper was signed: "Wilhelm Leonhardt, this 7th day of August, 1775."

"But how do you suppose Ziggner got this paper?" he asked.

Baum's brow furrowed. "Remember how you told me this Herr Crainter was found dead in a ditch off the King's Bridge Road? Well, I suspect he was carryin' it with him then. You said the servingman at the tavern told you this Crainter was a British agent. He must a' kept it rather than trust to the safety of any vault in wartime."

Steps sounded on the ladder, and Claus joined them. Wordless, he pressed Johann's hand. The boy clung to it a minute. But for that strong arm he might never have recovered his heritage!

"Think you're well enough to come up on deck?" asked Claus. "The wind seems to have died down. The sailors say the pump, since it was fixed this morning, has slowed the leak. They hope to rig a jury mast to help us on our way."

"Our way?" asked Johann. "Where are we going? I thought nobody aboard knew."

"Captain Kelle told us," said Claus. "When it seemed the *Triton* might founder last night, he revealed our orders were for Quebec. But he doesn't know what we were to do there. If we reach it in our present condition, we'll be lucky. The ship's captain told me just now we'd been blown so far south we're off the Delaware Capes. But come on, up with you."

On deck, spars broken and twisted in their cordage

lay thick about; there were great rents in the stout bulwarks, deep furrows in the worn decks where the cannon
had rolled. But the sun was trying to get through the
cloud rack blowing off rapidly to the west.

Just as the sun strove to clear the clouds, so some of
the crewmen were busy, coiling up tangled lines, tossing
overboard shattered bits of wood. Others were hard at
work fashioning a jury, or spare, mast. All about, soldiers who had lain for days in the hold, wretched and ill,
were standing or sitting, enjoying again the fresh, sparkling air.

The waves still tossed mightily, but now they were
not crested with angry, white tips. Even the *Triton* labored less now. She no longer fell into the trough of
every wave, nor did she take every sea over her battered
bow.

Johann stood a long time gazing at the rolling waters,
at the clouds racing by, at the now near, now far burst
of illumination on the dark green waves as the sun
struggled through. Claus and Baum stood silent by his
side.

Then he said quietly:

"Somehow now, I don't care whether I ever go back
to Cassel. My father, an outcast from his own land, came
to this New World and made himself liked and re-
spected—he must have to gain all the wealth he has left
me. He did it—not because he knew somebody or was
somebody's lackey. He had the chance to do it because,
I've found out, in this New World they don't ask who
you are. They take you for what you can do, and respect
you for it."

Johann paused, eyes still fixed to the west on the now dancing, shimmering waves. "I think," he continued, "he intended that I make a fresh start, too, away from the Old World, where men, because they have power at someone else's expense, can buy and sell others' lives."

"But what will you do?" asked Baum.

"Yes. I've thought of it too," chimed in Claus. "But what will we do?"

Silently, Johann reached out to grasp the hands nearest him.

"Why, we'll," and he emphasized the "we'll," "just have to wait—wait till this war is over." He halted again. "But it won't last much longer. I feel certain of that now. Those Americans have something, just as Zack, the farm boy, told me. I don't know what it is. But somehow, I feel we can't go wrong with them. We should have been fighting with them—not against them. Maybe, if we are lucky, they'll forgive us. They must know we didn't ask to go into battle against them. Maybe they'll take us in and let us be a part of the free country they're always telling about."

Behind him, Johann heard a sudden shout. The sailors were raising a tattered sail on the jury mast. The *Triton* was no longer a helpless, waterlogged wreck. She headed up into the wind, headed north once more.

Almost at the same time the soldiers on deck began reciting a familiar Psalm. Even the sailors, not understanding a word of what was being said slowly, solemnly, somehow caught the fervor in the words. Some bowed their heads. Others removed their rough sea

210

caps. The chorus rose higher against the slap of water, over the creaking of the old hull:

"For he commandeth, and raiseth the stormy wind, which lifteth up the waves thereof. They mount up to the heaven, they go down again to the depths: their soul is melted because of trouble. . . . Then they cry unto the Lord in their trouble, and he bringeth them out of their distresses. He maketh the storm a calm, so that the waves thereof are still. Then they are glad because they be quiet; so he bringeth them unto their desired haven."

The voices died away.

"Amen," murmured Baum and Claus together.

"Amen," whispered Johann, as he clutched the old watch tightly in his fist.

AUTHOR'S NOTE

BUT it wasn't as easy as Johann and his friends, Claus and Baum, thought. The *Triton,* slowly making its way back, was off the Delaware Capes when she was captured by two American privateers. The ship was brought into Little Egg Harbor, New Jersey, near the end of September, 1779, and the men taken again to Philadelphia, then finally to Reading, Pennsylvania.

Here Johann and his fellow prisoners remained until early in 1782 when they were released, active warfare having ended with Lord Cornwallis' surrender at Yorktown, Virginia, months before.

Although a prisoner for a second time, Johann found no reason to change his resolve to remain in America. Johann, Baum, and Claus were permitted to settle permanently in the new nation, as did many another Hessian when the long, cruel war was over.

With the funds left him by his father—found intact in the Water Street vault—Johann set up a small trading post in the foothills of the Alleghenies on the land mapped in the watch. He thus passed his remaining years aiding new settlers to get their start over the mountain barriers, into the newly opened western territory.